Helen Brooks

HIS CHRISTMAS BRIDE

D1238278

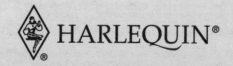

HARLEQUIN®

TORONTO • NEW YORK • LONDON
AMSTERDAM • PARIS • SYDNEY • HAMBURG
STOCKHOLM • ATHENS • TOKYO • MILAN • MADRID
PRAGUE • WARSAW • BUDAPEST • AUCKLAND

ISBN-13: 978-0-373-12689-7
ISBN-10:   0-373-12689-1

HIS CHRISTMAS BRIDE

First North American Publication 2007.

All about the author...
Helen Brooks

HELEN BROOKS was born and educated in
Northampton, England. She met her husband at the age
of sixteen and thirty-five years later, the magic is still
there. They have three lovely children and a menagerie
of animals in the house. The children, friends and
pets keep the house buzzing and the food cupboards
empty, but Helen wouldn't have it any other way.

Helen began writing in 1990 as she approached that
milestone of a birthday—forty! She realized that her
two teenage ambitions—writing a novel and learning
to drive—had been lost amid babies and family life,
so she set about resurrecting them. Her first novel
was accepted after one rewrite, and she passed her
driving test (the former was a joy and the latter an
unmitigated nightmare).

Being a committed Christian and fervent animal lover,
Helen finds that time is always at a premium, but
walking in the countryside with her husband and
dogs, meals out followed by the cinema or theater,
and reading, swimming and visiting with friends are
all fitted in somehow. She also enjoys sitting in her
wonderfully therapeutic, rambling old garden in the
sun, with a glass of red wine (under the guise of
resting while thinking, of course!).

Since becoming a full-time writer, Helen has found
her occupation one of pure joy. She loves exploring
what makes people tick, and finds the old adage
"truth is stranger than fiction" to be absolutely true.
She would love to hear from any readers, care of
Harlequin Presents®.

CHAPTER ONE

How could the room be reduced to this state when she had only been gone for a minute? Blossom White surveyed the scene in front of her, and tried to make herself heard above the rampaging infants. There might be only four of them but they were making enough noise for a couple of dozen children. 'Harry! Simone! That's *enough*. Stop throwing cake at Rebecca and Ella this instant.'

The twins ignored her and continued to pelt two-year-olds Rebecca and Ella—who appeared to be screaming with delight and not distress—with lumps of chocolate gateau.

Jolly Aunty Blossom went out of the window as a good dollop of gooey cake landed splat on her forehead. Forgetting she had promised herself that with her sister, the children's mother, in hospital she would be patience itself with her nephew and nieces, Blossom sprang across the room and seized the elder children in a firm grip.

Her fingers itching to smack small bottoms, Blossom contented herself with hissing ferociously, 'Did you hear what I said? That's enough. No TV after tea for you, now. You're straight to bed after your bath.'

'We want to watch our programmes.' Harry's angelic

face—which was all at odds with his volatile and difficult nature—frowned at her and he wriggled in her grasp.

'No deal, Harry. Not until you can do what you're told.'

'Mummy always lets us.'

Mummy no doubt lived in a state of perpetual exhaustion. 'I'm not your mummy, and *I* tell *you* what to do, not the other way round. Understand?'

This was clearly a new concept for her nephew, along with the other side to Aunty Blossom he was seeing, and he responded to it by erupting in a storm of tears, the three girls joining in after a startled moment or two.

How Melissa copes with two sets of twins under the age of five I just don't know, Blossom thought grimly. She had been in charge of them for one day and she felt like a wet rag. Glancing at the fragments of cake and cream splattered on Melissa's white walls, and the table swimming in spilt orange juice which was steadily dripping onto the varnished floorboards, Blossom contemplated the idea of joining in with the children and bawling her head off. Instead she said firmly, 'No more crying. We're going to clear this mess up together, Harry and Simone, OK? Who can clear up the most?'

'Me, me.' Harry's tears stopped like magic.

Sending the older two to fetch the kitchen cleaner and kitchen roll, Blossom stared at her younger nieces. They too had stopped crying and were engaged in licking their small hands clean of chocolate, giggling as bits continued to drop on the floor from their clothes and hair.

Whisking them up in her arms, Blossom carried the little girls into the sitting room where she popped them in their playpen until she could deal with them. She'd never agreed with the concept of playpens before Melissa had had the children, but now she was all for them. It might be a bit like putting a child in a cage, but she was now of the opinion it also kept hard-worked mothers sane.

Returning to the dining room, she found Harry and Simone busily clearing up. It took a while. Eventually, though, the room was restored to order, all four children had been bathed, read to and were asleep, and Blossom staggered downstairs for a cup of coffee. She had been trying to make one earlier while the children were occupied eating their tea—a big mistake.

Suddenly, after the mayhem of the day, she had a chance to sit and think, and she almost found herself wishing the children awake—*almost*. Ever since her brother-in-law Greg had called her that morning in a blind panic to say that Melissa had been rushed into hospital with terrible stomach pains, she had had her sister in the back of her mind whatever she'd done. Now all was quiet and still, fear for Melissa became paramount.

She had rushed to the house in a leafy suburb of Sevenoaks from her flat in London in record time early that morning, to find Greg tearing his hair out.

'She was all right last night,' he'd said desperately, meeting her at the front door with Rebecca and Ella in his arms, and Harry and Simone just behind him, a slice of buttered toast in each of their sticky hands. 'And then she woke about three, saying she felt sick, and half an hour later the pain kicked in. Within a short while she couldn't stand or move, she was so bad. The doctor thinks it might be her appendix. He says it can happen like that sometimes, with no warning whatsoever.'

'Well, I'm here now, and I'm staying until I'm not needed,' Blossom said firmly. 'You get off to the hospital and forget everything here.'

He'd gone like a shot but, Blossom reflected ruefully now,

she hadn't meant he forget them so completely he didn't let her know what was happening. Reaching for the telephone at her elbow, she called the hospital, and after being transferred twice she eventually spoke to a Sister Pearson, who informed her very kindly that Melissa was at present in Theatre. 'Mr Robinson, the consultant in charge of your sister, thinks she may have suffered a severe attack of appendicitis, and that the appendix might possibly have ruptured. He felt an operation to find out what was what was the safest option.' The Sister paused. 'I'm afraid your brother-in-law is a little…tense at the moment. Shall I get him to ring you later, once your sister is out of Theatre, and he can give you some news?'

'That'd be great, thanks.' Blossom replaced the receiver and reached for her coffee. She could imagine Sister Pearson was mistress of the understatement. Greg would be climbing the walls, no doubt. He was a brilliant physicist with a top job in a major electronic firm in London, but on a practical, day-to-day level absolutely useless. Highly strung and mind-blowingly academic, he barely existed in the real world. But ever since he and her sister had set eyes on each other at university they had been inseparable. That Greg relied on Melissa utterly and completely was indisputable; he wouldn't know what day it was unless she told him. She was his sun, moon and stars.

Oh, Melissa, Melissa. Blossom leant forward, the mug of coffee in her hands and her eyes tightly shut. She had to be all right, she just had to be. Anything else was unthinkable. Although not identical twins, Blossom and Melissa were nevertheless very close, in spite of Melissa having married Greg at the age of twenty-two and moved here. Blossom, on the other hand, had chosen the career path and stayed in

London, carving a hard-won niche for herself as a freelance fashion photographer after years of blood, sweat and toil.

Blossom raised her head and glanced mistily round the sitting room, before reaching for her handkerchief. It wouldn't be fair if anything happened to Melissa now, not when she had finally got the family she had waited for for so long. Right from their honeymoon Greg and her sister had tried for a baby, but Melissa had endured one miscarriage after another. She and Greg had spent a fortune going to the best doctors, both abroad and at home, but as the years had crept by they had eventually accepted it was just going to be the two of them. And then Melissa had found herself pregnant with twins just after their seventh anniversary, and lo and behold Rebecca and Ella had followed twenty months later. In spite of the timing, Melissa had been ecstatic.

Telling herself she couldn't give way to the flood of tears threatening to burst forth, Blossom forced herself to go into the kitchen to make a sandwich. She had eaten nothing all day, and her stomach was still twisted in a giant knot, but she was feeling distinctly lightheaded now. It wouldn't do to be anything but one-hundred-per-cent fit if one of the children woke up and needed her. Especially if it was Harry.

She reached for the loaf of bread in the bread bin—home-made. She didn't know how her sister did it, but Melissa insisted she wanted the children to have nothing but good, home-made produce every day. She had just set it on the kitchen table when the doorbell rang. No more than a second later, it rang again.

Worried it would wake Harry, who was the lightest of sleepers, Blossom galloped to the front door, mentally cursing whoever was standing on the doorstep. Wings she didn't have!

'Hi there.'

He had dark hair, the bluest of blue eyes and a tall, lean frame that seemed to go on for ever. Six-foot-four at least, Blossom thought inconsequentially. Maybe six-five. Suddenly she was vitally aware that she was in her oldest jeans, and that her white shirt bore evidence of everything the children had eaten during the day. And she hadn't stopped to put any make-up on that morning. Or do anything with her hair other than drag it back in a ponytail. 'Hello,' she managed weakly. 'Can I help?'

'I'm Zak Hamilton.' He extended a tanned hand which emerged from the crisp sleeve of a pristine clean and definitely designer-cut pale blue shirt which had never come within a mile of grubby little hands and mouths. Neither had his immaculate pale-grey trousers, come to that. 'Greg works for me?' he added helpfully as Blossom continued to gaze at him.

Zak Hamilton. Of course. This was the big boss of Hamilton Electronics. She remembered Melissa saying the son had inherited the company six years ago, when the father had died unexpectedly, and that since then it had mushroomed into a huge giant of a success. Zak Hamilton had the Midas touch, Melissa had stated, partly due to the fact that he was intimidatingly intelligent and forward thinking, but also because he wasn't afraid to take a risk now and again. It had been he who had head-hunted Greg within months of inheriting the firm, making him an offer he couldn't refuse. She also remembered she'd got the impression Melissa wasn't very fond of Greg's boss, although her sister hadn't actually said so. Greg, on the other hand, couldn't speak highly enough of him. He sang his praises all the time.

Pulling herself together, Blossom said, 'I'm Melissa's

sister, Greg's sister-in-law.' And then felt slightly idiotic. Of course she was Greg's sister-in-law if she was his wife's sister. Any fool could have worked that out, and this man was no fool.

'Hi, Greg's sister-in-law.' He looked amused. 'Do you have a name as well as that title?'

Here we go. She just hated telling anyone her name for the first time, but especially this man somehow. 'Blossom White.' She waited for the blue eyes to register surprise and for his amusement to increase. Neither happened. Instead he continued to survey her steadily. 'Melissa and I are twins,' she added hurriedly. 'Although we don't look it. Our mother thought it kind of cute to call the elder twin, my sister, Melissa—which means "bee"—and the younger Blossom. The bee going to the blossom, you know? She thought the elder would look after the younger, I guess.' *The number of times she'd explained this.*

'Did it work?' he asked with what seemed genuine interest.

'Not really.' It was more the other way round, if anything. Melissa had always been the shy, retiring one whereas Blossom rushed in where angels feared to tread. Well, until Dean, that was. She had changed a lot since then—in her private life, at least. In her work she had to be as loud and confident as ever. Aware he was still staring at her—probably thinking what a gawky mess she was compared to Melissa, who was always beautifully turned out in spite of the children—Blossom said, 'You've come to ask how things are?' Another daft question in the circumstances.

He nodded. 'Greg was going to call, but he hasn't.'

'I can't tell you much, except Melissa is having an operation and I'm waiting for Greg to call to say how things went.'

'An operation?'

He looked concerned, genuinely concerned, and to Blossom's horror she felt her nose prick and the tears she had banished earlier bank up behind her eyes. 'They...they think her appendix might have burst or something.' *Don't cry. Whatever you do, don't cry.* Not now. Not in front of him.

'I'm so sorry; I didn't realise it was serious.' His voice was rich, deep, and carried the slightest of accents which she couldn't place. 'Can I do anything to help at all?'

Taking a deep breath, she realised she'd been terribly rude in not asking him in, which wasn't like her. Mind, she didn't *feel* like herself with Melissa perhaps at death's door. 'No, everything is under control,' she lied politely. 'But perhaps you'd like to come in for a coffee or something?'

'Thanks.'

He didn't hesitate. Blossom admitted to being a little taken aback. He must realise she'd had a day of it from the way she looked, surely, and that she wanted nothing more than a hot bath? But perhaps he assumed she always looked like something the cat wouldn't deign to drag in. 'You'll have to excuse the state of me,' she said somewhat stiffly as she led the way into the sitting room, remembering too late she hadn't got round to cleaning the playpen after Rebecca and Ella had gone to sleep. 'The children had a battle with chocolate cake.' She indicated the state of the play pen with a wave of her hand. 'As you can see.'

He nodded thoughtfully. 'I wondered what it was on your forehead. Obviously the chocolate cake won.'

Well, that wasn't very tactful. She forced a tight smile, reminding herself this man was Greg's boss. 'I'm not used to looking after four young children,' she said in a voice that was just off-frosty. 'And Harry's something of a handful.'

He nodded again. She didn't know if it was a 'that's pretty obvious' nod, or a 'poor you' nod, but she rather suspected the former. That being the case—and especially because he was standing there looking like he had just stepped out of a top magazine for the well-dressed man—her voice remained at the same temperature when she said, 'If you'll excuse me a minute, I'll see about the coffee.' And left the room with as much dignity as she could muster in the appalling circumstances.

Once in the hall, she shut the sitting-room door firmly behind her and then darted into the downstairs cloakroom. Looking into the small round mirror, she groaned softly.

It was as bad as it could be. Wild, scarecrow hair, shiny pink face—except for the bits smeared with chocolate cake—and she even had a couple of leaves from the weeping-willow tree lodged in her hair, from when she had romped with Harry and the girls in the garden before tea. She had been trying to tire the four of them out before bedtime but in the event the only person who had nearly collapsed with exhaustion was her.

'Great, just great,' she muttered at the scowling reflection in the glass. And then she shrugged. What did it matter how she looked with Melissa so ill? Zak Hamilton would have to take her as he found her. She would give him his cup of coffee and then politely make it clear she expected him to leave.

In spite of herself, though, she found she couldn't leave the cloakroom without washing her hands and face, and brushing her hair with the brush Melissa kept in the cabinet for when the children needed quickly sprucing up. Looping her hair back into a ponytail that was now sleek and shiny, she quickly checked herself once more and then made her way to the kitchen.

Instant coffee would have to do. She reached for the jar she had bought herself on her last visit to the house two months before, when she had babysat the children over a weekend while Melissa and Greg had gone to Paris for their wedding anniversary. She had been too shattered coping with the children to bother with the coffee-maker, and she saw now the coffee hadn't been used since. Melissa was the original earth-mother; 'instant' didn't feature in her sister's vocabulary. It made up the main content of hers.

She had just spooned a generous amount into two china mugs festooned with poppies when the telephone rang. Snatching up the kitchen phone, she said breathlessly, 'Yes?'

'Blossom? It's Greg. She's out of Theatre, and the consul-tant is happy with how things went. The appendix was on the point of bursting, so it's as well he operated immediately. She'll be in a few days, though. Something to do with her blood.'

'Oh, Greg.' Blossom found she had to sit down fairly quickly on one of the stools at the breakfast bar, her ears ringing. 'Have you spoken to her? How is she feeling?'

'She's out of it, will be till morning, according to the staff. In spite of that I think I'd like to hang round a bit longer, if that's OK with you? Can you cope with the kids?'

He sounded so lost and shaken, Blossom's heart went out to him. 'Of course,' she said. 'You stay as long as you want. The kids are fine and they're all asleep. Have you eaten anything?'

'Eaten?' he repeated vaguely. 'Oh, yes, I think so. Some sandwiches. Look, I have to go. I'll see you in the morning.' And he put the phone down. Typical Greg.

'You OK? I heard the phone. Was it the hospital?'

The quiet voice from the kitchen doorway brought Blossom's head up. Zak was standing there, his blue eyes narrowed. It was a totally inappropriate moment to register that he had to be one of the most handsome men she had ever set eyes on. She gulped, then said, 'That was Greg. Melissa's out of Theatre, and everything went well. She's sleeping off the anaesthetic.'

He nodded. 'Good. Now I'm going to ask you what you just asked Greg—have you eaten anything?'

She stared at him. 'It's been too hectic.'

He nodded again. 'You look like death warmed up,' he said bluntly. 'You're not going to faint on me, are you?'

He had a nerve. Adrenalin pumped a healthy dose of anger into her wilting limbs. She knew she looked awful, he needn't rub it in. 'I'm perfectly all right,' she said coldly. 'Thank you. And I have never fainted in my life.'

It was as though she hadn't spoken. 'Why don't you go and have a bath while I order some food in?' he said in a tone which made it more of an order than a suggestion. 'I haven't eaten yet, and I'm starving. What do you prefer—Indian, Chinese, Italian, Thai? My treat. I insist.'

He could have grown two heads from the way Blossom was staring at him. Talk about taking charge, she thought resentfully.

It took her a few seconds before she could say, 'I don't think so, but thanks anyway.' She hoped he'd take the hint.

'You'll be perfectly safe.' The smoky voice now held a definite thread of dark amusement. 'I'm not about to take advantage of the situation, if that's what's worrying you.'

Blossom wondered what it was about 'I don't think so' that he didn't understand. Drawing on her limited store of patience, which the day with the children had seriously depleted, she slid off the stool, saying, 'I didn't think that for a moment.'

It was true, she hadn't. Zak Hamilton looked like the sort of man who chose his women for the wow factor they'd present when seen out on his arm. Even when she had her glad rags on and was all made up she wouldn't qualify. She just didn't want to play the part of the needy recipient in his Good Samaritan scenario, that was all, not when he had made it clear she looked pretty dire to him. Even with the temptation of Thai food. She loved Thai cooking.

'Good. What's it to be, then? I rather favour Thai, but I am open to suggestions.'

She had a very good suggestion for him and it wasn't anything to do with food. 'Look, Mr Hamilton, I don't want to appear rude…' she said coolly, reminding herself yet again he *was* Greg's boss and the owner of the firm to boot. 'But I have got things to do. Now, if you'd like that coffee before you go?'

Cornflower-blue eyes held her dark brown ones. 'You're not the easiest of females to get on with, are you?' he observed mildly. 'Definitely a bit prickly round the edges.'

Actually, she could get on with absolutely everyone, everybody said so. 'I'll tell Greg you called by to see how Melissa was,' she said icily. *So now clear off, Mr Big-Boss Hamilton!*

'Actually, I didn't.' He was leaning against the doorframe, arms folded and expression benign. 'Call to see how Melissa was, that is.'

'But you said that's why you had come.' Hadn't he?

'You asked me if I'd called round to see how things were, that's slightly different.' He looked at her from steady eyes.

Not in her book. It was exactly the same.

'I didn't realise your sister was in hospital; Greg merely mentioned his wife had been taken ill with stomach trouble to my secretary when he phoned this morning. I imagined she'd eaten something that had disagreed with her, something like that. I called round to make sure Greg remembered we have an important meeting in Watford tomorrow morning.'

Blossom glared at him. 'My sister is lying in a hospital bed after an emergency operation, and you expect him to go with you to a meeting in Watford?' Her voice had risen with each word. What was with this man? Had he no feelings at all?

He sighed. 'I told you, I didn't know the circumstances,' he said with exaggerated patience. 'Of course I don't expect him to accompany me now. I wouldn't dream of it, in fact.'

Slightly mollified, Blossom tipped boiling water into the two poppy mugs. 'Milk and sugar?' she asked him without looking at the doorway again.

'I take mine black.'

She had rather thought he might. And he would take ten-mile runs as a matter of course before breakfast, and drive a snazzy, top-of-the-range sportscar, and always sleep in the buff on black linen sheets. This last thought was more than a little disconcerting. Blossom took her time adding sugar and milk to her own mug, so the pink in her cheeks had subsided a little when she handed Zak his coffee, making sure their hands didn't touch.

'Thanks.' He straightened up from the wall with animal grace. Her tummy did a funny little kind of hop, skip and jump.

'Would you like a biscuit or a piece of cake with that?' After refusing the offer of a meal—especially as he had mentioned he hadn't eaten and was starving—she felt politeness necessitated the offer. Besides which, her stomach was rumbling and demanding food—another moment and he'd hear it.

'What kind of cake? It's not the remains of the chocolate one, is it?' he asked, straight-faced.

He was laughing at her, even if it didn't show. For answer, Blossom opened the cupboard and brought out Melissa's cake tins, leaving the one containing the other half of the chocolate gateau on the shelf. His loss. She'd picked up a morsel from the table when she had been helping the twins clear up, and it was absolutely delicious. Mind you, the fruit cake and fat ginger-and-walnut cake the other tins held looked fantastic too, but then everything Melissa made was wonderful.

'I'll have a piece of that one, please.' He pointed to the ginger-and-walnut cake. 'Did you make these?'

Any of her friends would have collapsed with laughter if they had heard that. 'I don't cook,' she said briefly. 'These are ones Melissa's baked.' She cut a generous portion, placed it on one of Melissa's china teaplates and handed it to him before doing the same for herself. 'Shall we go through to the sitting room?' Funny, but since he had appeared in the doorway the kitchen seemed to have shrunk to half its size and was far too intimate. 'We can sit in comfort in there.'

Once in the sitting room, Zak seated himself on the sofa. Blossom made sure she took the armchair furthest away from it. After taking a king-size bite of cake, he pronounced it delicious and then eyed her lazily. 'So, you don't cook.' One black eyebrow quirked. 'What do you do?'

'I'm sorry?' He was laughing at her again, she just knew it.

'Your job—or don't you work?' he asked smoothly.

'Yes, I work.' He was rattling her, but she didn't want to give him the satisfaction of knowing it. Drawing in a deep, hidden breath, she told herself to relax before she proffered, 'I'm a fashion photographer, actually.' *Make of that what you will.*

The eyebrow rose higher. 'Really?'

Yes, really, in spite of my present attire. She forced herself to smile. ''Fraid so.' She took several sips of coffee and then decided to play him at his own game. 'Do you find that surprising?' she asked sweetly. *Agree if you dare.*

'Yes, I do.' He eyed her expressionlessly.

This guy took the biscuit, he really did, but he could darn well spell it out. 'Why is that, Mr Hamilton?'

'Zak, please.' He had the gall to smile. 'No formality.'

That smile. Perfect white teeth. She bet he had never endured the mortification of the braces and dental work which had hampered her teenage years. 'Why is that, Zak?' she asked with grim civility. Greg's income depended on this man.

'You say you and Melissa are twins, but from what I've seen, and more especially from what Greg says, Melissa is the epitome of the contented wife and mother without a career bone in her body. I thought twins were supposed to be the same.'

She stared at him. 'We're twins,' she pointed out. 'Not clones.' Why was it men like him always had the sort of wicked, lusciously thick eyelashes women would kill to possess? It gave them an unfair advantage. Dean's had been an inch long.

'Point taken.' He grinned and took another huge bite of Melissa's yummy cake. 'This is absolutely fantastic, by the way.'

Blossom silently pondered whether she would have preferred him to say he had been surprised because she looked the exact opposite of anything remotely fashionable. Probably not.

'So, fashion photography.' He had finished the cake in record time. 'Tough field to break into, I'd imagine. Do you work for a studio or fashion house or magazine?'

Blossom shook her head. 'I'm a freelance photographer; I prefer it that way. And yes, it was tough to get into, and is just as tough to continue in, but I like it. I guess I have a knack of selling my techniques and the pictures I produce, though, that helps. There's lots of excellent photographers who don't know how to market their skills.'

He nodded. Settling back on the sofa, he crossed one leg over the other after draining the mug of coffee, his arms along the back of the seat. It was a very masculine pose. Blossom ignored the quickening of her heartbeat as grey cloth pulled tight over hard male thighs. She tried to think of something to say to fill the silence and failed miserably, gulping at her coffee instead. Suddenly she wasn't at all hungry.

'So.' The piercing eyes were tight on her face. 'No husband around?' He nodded at her left hand, which was devoid of rings.

Blossom felt the question in the pit of her stomach, which was ridiculous. She was well past that stage. Before tonight she hadn't thought of Dean in days, and when she had it had been with acute loathing. Her voice crisp, she said, 'No, there's no husband, and isn't likely to be. That's another area Melissa and I differ in.' She raised her chin a fraction of an inch.

'Right.' The blue eyes narrowed. 'That taken as read, do you fancy going for a drink one evening?'

Surprise robbed Blossom of speech. It was the last thing she'd expected, and for a moment she wasn't sure if she'd heard him correctly. He wasn't interested in her, surely? He was the sort of man who would definitely go for a certain type—a tall, willowy blonde or vivacious redhead, the sort of female who would cause the conversation to lull whenever they entered a room—and she didn't fit the bill. She wouldn't crack any mirrors, admittedly, but she wasn't particularly tall or small, just average. Her brown hair and eyes were pretty average too. Melissa had been the one to get the looks. At five-feet-ten, with liquid brown eyes and natural ash-blonde hair, her twin was a stunner. Not that Melissa was vain, just the opposite.

Without considering her words, Blossom blurted, 'Sorry, but I don't date. I made up my mind years ago that I'm a career

girl, and romance and getting to the top in any profession
don't mix. Not for women, at least.'

He straightened slightly. 'If you're saying a woman can't
have a love life as well as a top job, I disagree. This is the
twenty-first century, not the dark ages.'

'I'm aware of that.' She agreed with him, but wasn't about
to say so. The excuse she'd used could very well be the
coward's way out but it had sufficed in the past to put men
off. She wasn't about to bare her soul to any man, especially
Greg's boss. Besides, she had the feeling he was the kind of
guy who would be persistent when it came to getting his own
way unless he was satisfied there was no chance whatsoever.
And there was not. Not with her. The last thing she needed
was a Zak type.

'Another piece of cake?' The silence was stretching on and
becoming uncomfortable. She did so hope he would say no.

'Thanks, I'd love one.' He held out his plate. She noticed
with a pang of what could have been pique that he wasn't
particularly devastated she was off the menu. He was probably
the sort of male who felt compelled to try his luck with
any unattached female below a certain age, she thought
maliciously. Date them, persuade them to fall for him, and
when the challenge was gone move on to the next poor sop.
But perhaps she was just being hideously unfair. She knew
Dean had soured her. Mind, she doubted Zak Hamilton would
go to the trouble some men did to get a woman into bed—he
wouldn't have to, for one thing. Dean had been a head-turner,
but Greg's boss was in a different league altogether. As he very
well knew, no doubt.

Becoming aware she was staring at him, Blossom hastily
reached for the proferred plate. 'Another coffee?' she offered

for good measure, feeling a little guilty about her uncharitable thoughts—although they were probably all bang on the mark.

'Great.' He settled back against the billowy sofa with every appearance of relaxed enjoyment. 'And make the cake a big slice, would you? I'm starving.'

Cheeky hound. Blossom smiled frostily. Utterly sure of himself and arrogant with it—just the sort of male she'd walk a mile to avoid. Still, she'd offered seconds now.

Once in the kitchen she made the coffee and cut a generous wedge of cake—not that the other slice had been small, she thought grimly. She looked at the half of cake remaining in the tin, and for a moment was tempted to put that on his plate rather than the slice she'd cut. She resisted. Less because he was Greg's boss and more because he'd probably eat it quite happily, remaining oblivious to any sarcasm. Giant ego.

Walking through to the sitting room, she silently handed him the plate and mug, deciding the cool, non-speaking approach was the quickest way to get rid of him. No more repartee.

'Thanks.' He took the cake with boyish enthusiasm. 'Your sister is some cook. She didn't strike me as the sort of woman who would bake her own cake when I met her at Christmas.'

The work do. Blossom had babysat on that occasion too, and she remembered Melissa had looked like every man's fantasy with bells on in the draped-silk jersey dress with plunging neckline she had worn. Talk about stereotyping! Blossom eyed him severely. 'My sister is extremely domesticated,' she said coolly. 'All Melissa ever wanted from when she was a child was to be a wife and mother, and she does both extremely well.'

'And you disapprove of that?' he asked evenly.

'No, I do not.' Coolness went out of the window and she

glared at him. 'Of course I don't. Everyone, man and woman, should follow their own path. We've chosen very different ones, that's all. I wouldn't dream of expecting Melissa to want what I want. We respect each other as individuals.'

'Greg's crazy about her, isn't he?'

'She's crazy about him.'

Zak's nod was thoughtful. 'He's something of a mad professor, but brilliant, quite brilliant. I can see it would suit him to have someone to look after him.'

She couldn't imagine Zak wanting to be looked after. Blossom sipped at her now-cool coffee as she watched him eat the second slice of cake. It was gone in a few big bites. He ate with relish; she could imagine he was a man who tackled every area of his life with the same unabashed gusto. Something in the pit of her stomach curled, and she lowered her eyes to her empty mug. When she raised them, Zak was looking straight at her.

'You're clearly wiped out, I'd better be going,' he said softly. He stood to his feet. 'Thanks for the coffee and cake.'

Flustered, Blossom rose a moment later, furious that her cheeks had turned pink when there was no logical reason for it. 'I'll let Greg know you called by when he comes home.'

'Tell him I won't expect him in until Melissa's home and feeling herself again while you're at it,' he said lazily as she led the way to the front door. 'There is nothing brewing in the pipeline that can't keep for a week or two.'

'Right.' She nodded. She felt ridiculously out of her depth. What was it about this man that made her feel she'd regressed to the painful teenage years, when she'd been gawky, awkward and tongue-tied? Whatever it was, she could do without it. She opened the front door and stood aside for him to exit the house. Instead he stopped in front of her.

His eyes unfathomable, he murmured, 'It's been nice meeting you. Do I take it you'll be sticking around for a day or two?'

It was a simple question, so why the agitation in her breast? 'Until I'm not needed,' she confirmed. 'It's the least I can do.'

'That won't prove difficult work-wise?'

She shook her head. 'As luck would have it, I've just finished a pretty extensive spell of work and had promised myself a break.'

'We might see each other again, then. If anything crops up I need to speak to Greg about.' He smiled a slow smile.

He was the head of a major electronics firm and he was talking about face-to-face contact? Without pausing to consider how it sounded, she said, 'Have you got Greg's mobile number?'

He continued to regard her for another moment before his eyes crinkled at the corners. 'Do I take that as a polite way of saying I wouldn't be welcome?' he asked mildly.

The pink in her cheeks had turned to a fiery red that would have rivalled a boiled lobster. Her embarrassment wasn't helped by the fact that he seemed to find her amusing rather than offensive. 'Of course not,' she said tightly. 'I was just checking you could contact him if you needed to, that's all.'

'Just checking.' Two words, but they carried a huge amount of disbelief.

'Absolutely.' She stared straight back into the blue eyes.

'Right.' His tone had not changed. He held her gaze for one more eternal moment, and then stepped out of the house and walked towards a low-slung sportscar parked at the side of the pebbled front garden. It was a beauty, an Aston Martin, in a delicate shade of silver grey, gleaming in the summer twilight.

Blossom wondered why she hadn't noticed it when he had

arrived, and wouldn't admit it was because she'd had eyes for nothing but him. She shut the front door, not waiting to see him drive away, and then stood leaning against it as she strained her ears. There was the sound of a car door shutting, the throb of a powerful engine and then the scrunchy noise of tyres on stone. He was leaving, so why was her heart still thudding?

It was only when all was quiet that she became aware she had been holding her breath. Letting it out in a great sigh, she straightened. That was that. He had gone. Undoubtedly with the impression that Melissa's twin sister was a cold, hard and somewhat rude career woman without a romantic bone in the whole of her body.

'And I'm not.' She spoke aloud into the quiet, slumbering hall where the only sound was the steady ticking of the magnificent antique grandfather clock in the far corner. Was it her imagination, or was it staring at her with a reproachful look on its superior face?

Blossom stuck out her tongue in a manner which belied her thirty-four years, resolving to put Zak Hamilton and his possible opinion of her out of her mind. She had more than enough to cope with as it was in the forseeable future; the whirling dervish that was her nephew would be waking at the crack of dawn, if the weekend she'd babysat Melissa's children before was anything to go by. And, once Harry was awake, the world had no choice but to follow.

She squared her shoulders, breathed in and out very deeply, and made her way into the sitting room to clear away the mugs and plates.

CHAPTER TWO

ANNOYINGLY, once Blossom was lying under the tastefully scented, crisp linen sheets in the generous double bed in Melissa's guest room, sleep became an impossibility. She found herself embroiled in a minute-by-minute post-mortem of the whole day, right from when Greg had first called her.

The crazy dash to the house, Greg's poor little wan face, the frantic pace that had ensued with the children, not to mention the mistakes she'd made in dealing with Harry—and overall the awful knowledge that her sister was in terrible pain and she couldn't help her. That had been excruciating.

Finally, when she couldn't keep him at bay a moment longer, she allowed Zak Hamilton to walk through the door of her mind. This resulted in a distinctly harrowing, squirmingly hot and embarrassing twenty minutes when she replayed every word he had said and she had said, every gesture, every look. She did this several times. More than several. It got worse, not better.

When she couldn't stand it a moment longer, Blossom slid out of bed and walked into the *en suite*, running herself a hot bath and adding a liberal amount of bath oil which magically promised to soothe and calm in equal measures. Stripping off the practical 'I'm dealing with children' pyjamas she had bought especially for her last babysitting endeavour, she surveyed herself in the full-length mirror to one side of the deep cast-iron bath before climbing into the perfumed water.

Only someone as effortlessly slim as Melissa could think having a mirror you couldn't avoid when you were naked was a good idea, she reflected ruefully as she inched her bottom slowly into water which seemed to be a good few degrees hotter than she had thought. Not that she was a two-ton Tessie by any means. She just wasn't naturally willowy like her sister.

She was now resting on the bottom of the bath, and breathed out thankfully. It had been obvious from an early age she took totally after their mother, whereas Melissa had inherited their father's to-die-for genes. Yet it had been apparent to anyone within a five-mile radius of their parents that their father had worshipped the ground his sweet but homely wife walked on.

Blossom's face took on a tender quality. She was so glad her parents had lived long enough to see Harry and Simone before they had been killed in a multiple car-crash three months after the twins had been born. They'd been so thrilled Melissa had achieved her heart's desire. She and Melissa had had the best of childhoods, and their parents had continued to be utterly supportive even after she and her sister had left home—Melissa to married life, and Blossom to follow her career in London. She had always dreamed she'd find a relationship similar to the one her parents had had one day, a love which would lead to marriage, perhaps even children, whilst her career was put on hold for a short time.

And then, a few months after her parents had died, Dean had come along just when she'd been beginning to doubt there would ever be a Mr Right among all the Mr Wrongs she'd dated in the past. She hadn't known then that, if all the Mr Wrongs in the world had been gathered up into one bundle, they wouldn't be as wrong as Dean had been.

Blossom tried to close her mind against the memories now pouring in, but it was too late; she had opened Pandora's box.

They had met at a fashion shoot; he had been one of the male models, and she had been bowled over by his dark Latin looks and smouldering charm. As he had intended she should be.

They had married two months to the day they had met, and already her photographs had begun to open doors for him. She had established good contacts over the years, and she had used every last one of them for Dean. He was her husband, her love; there was nothing she wouldn't have done for him.

She had been so looking forward to their first Christmas together. Blossom clenched her teeth as the pictures in her mind rolled on with relentless accuracy. On the day before Christmas Eve she had come home to the flat—her flat; Dean had been sharing a grotty bedsit with a friend called Julian when they had met. She found all his clothes and belongings gone and a note waiting for her, propped inappropriately—or perhaps completely appropriately, she thought bitterly— against their wedding photograph. A small, neatly folded piece of paper.

He was holidaying in the Caribbean, Dean had written. He would not be returning to the flat when he came back to England. Their marriage had been a terrible mistake. It was better they faced it now than later. This was all for the best, and he hoped she understood. *They had been married for seven months.*

It had got worse. Oh, how it had got worse.

When she had gone to the bank after Christmas it was to discover Dean had withdrawn every last penny from their joint savings account, which had housed her half of the inheritance from her parents' estate. A tidy nest-egg. All gone.

A week later a concerned work colleague had reported he had heard whispers Dean had taken someone with him to the Caribbean. Subsequent enquiries had revealed the woman had in fact been living with him in the bedsit when Blossom had met him—'Julian' was 'Juliette', and the two had never stopped seeing each other.

It had been a bitter pill to swallow, but Blossom had had to accept Dean had married her purely for the size of her bank account, and the influential circles within the modelling and TV fraternity she could introduce him to. His career—due mainly to her efforts on his behalf, along with the cash she had lavished on him for anything he had needed—had taken off far better than even he could have hoped for. He'd begun to fly high, and he and his Juliette must have been congratulating themselves at Blossom's gullibility as they had basked in the warm Caribbean sun, laughing at her as they'd sipped their cocktails.

She had been ill for some time after that.

Blossom moved restlessly in the warm water, drawing a mental veil over the emotional devastation she had suffered. *But what doesn't kill you makes you stronger*. She nodded to the thought which had been voiced by Greg, of all people. He had been right. When she had surfaced from the blanket of grief and despair, she found she'd become curiously autonomous, and she welcomed it. She never, *ever* wanted to put her trust on the line again. Her heart was her own, and she intended it would continue to remain so.

She understood work. Work was safe, secure, sure, even taking into account the inevitable backstabbing and diva-like skirmishes which were part and parcel of the fashion world. That world could be irritating, false and cruel; it could make her angry or plain disgusted on occasion. But the ups more than made up for the downs and, more importantly, even the worse aspects didn't touch the inner core of her. Didn't make her feel as though life wasn't worth living, that she was the ugliest, most unattractive, unworthy female since the beginning of creation. A man had done that, and she never intended to give another male the same opportunity. Once bitten, definitely twice shy.

Her mouth tightening, she stood up, reaching for the fluffy bath sheet and wrapping it round her. Why was she thinking about Dean tonight, reliving it all? She had thought that was behind her. It wasn't as though she cared about him any more.

Zak Hamilton. The name popped up as an answer all by itself. Blossom frowned. Over her dead body. She wouldn't give a man like Zak the tiniest chance of entering her life. But—the frown deepened—he *had* unsettled her. Rattled her. She didn't know why, but he had. And it wasn't his looks or wealth; she came into contact with plenty of drop-dead-gorgeous men in her line of work, and more than a few were well-heeled. Nothing like that intimidated or impressed her any more.

So—what was it about Zak she didn't like? His confidence, which definitely bordered on arrogance? The fact that he was probably one of the most handsome men she'd ever seen, and certainly possessed a male charisma that was dynamite? The way he'd looked at her, the amusement in his eyes, along with the fact he had made her feel like an insect under a microscope? A bumbling, somewhat ineffectual insect at that.

His manner, which had spoken of unlimited wealth and the knowledge people would jump as high as he ordered them to?

Dropping the sheet, she pulled on the pyjamas again and then rubbed the bottom of her shoulder-length hair with the handtowel. It had got slightly wet as she had lain in the bath.

She was probably being monumentally unfair, because she really knew nothing at all about Zak Hamilton, but she didn't care. She didn't like him. The brown-haired reflection in the mirror stared back at her, and as though it contradicted her she said firmly, 'I don't. Not one iota.'

Padding into the bedroom, she climbed into bed and was asleep within a minute or two.

The next days were hectic, but by the time Melissa came home Blossom felt she had got a handle on running a home and caring for four energetic and high-spirited little ones. Admittedly she hadn't attempted to bake—she knew her limits—but she had learnt how to manage Harry, and that was an accolade for anyone. The house was spick and span, she was up to date with the washing as well as the ironing, she'd even found time to cut the lawns and weed the flowerbeds. The children had been fed well on Melissa's cooking—courtesy of the well-stocked freezer—and had fully accepted Blossom after the somewhat disastrous first day.

'Thank you so much for holding the fort, everything looks lovely,' Melissa said gratefully once the initial hullabaloo caused by the children having their mother home again had died down. 'I feel positively guilty, having spent hours in bed watching TV and reading books in that lovely room at the hospital.' Courtesy of Greg's handsome private-health package at work.

'It was a pleasure.' Well, parts of it had been. Things such as reading Rebecca and Ella their bedtime story, when the two little girls had been damp and sweet-smelling from their bath and curled up sleepily beside her. Wrestling the rake off Harry when he'd snuck into the garden shed while her back had been turned hadn't been so hot. Her nephew had been intent on terrorising his sisters with it, and hadn't taken kindly to his fun being spoilt.

'Were they good?' Melissa turned fond eyes on her little brood, who were playing with Greg in the garden while the two sisters had a welcome cup of coffee. Fresh ground, now Melissa was home. She wouldn't dare to suggest anything else.

'Angelic,' Blossom lied stoutly. *Some of the time*.

'I bet you can't wait to get back to your flat and your own way of doing things,' Melissa said. 'Peace and quiet for hours on end if you want it.'

Blossom knew her sister didn't mean a word of it. Melissa couldn't think of a more wonderful existence than being with her children, and she expected everyone else to feel the same. Surprisingly—and she admitted this with a very real feeling of astonishment—Blossom knew she was really going to miss her nieces and nephew when she left. She loved them very much, of course, she always had, but over the last days she had begun to thoroughly enjoy their company and she hadn't expected that. They were funny and cute, and naughty and exhausting, but overall so *alive*, so brimming with wonder and excitement about the most ordinary things. And it kind of rubbed off on her, she'd found.

'Harry found a stone with a face in it this morning,' she said vaguely, her eyes intent on the children. 'He's wrapped it up as a present for you later, so make a big thing of it when he gives it to you, won't you?'

'Of course,' Melissa said softly, taking her twin's hand and squeezing it tight as she added, 'You're a star, sis, but you don't have to stay any longer if it's making things difficult with your work.'

'It isn't.' That was the truth, but even if work had been piling up to the ceiling she wouldn't have left. She had been shocked at how pale and washed out Melissa was. The doctors had discovered she was severely anaemic on top of having her appendix out. The result of having two sets of twins within twenty months of each other probably. Whatever, she intended to stay at least another week or so, and make sure Melissa had plenty of rest and sleep. She'd try and fit in a talk about not having to be superwoman all the time too if there was a suitable opportunity. The children wouldn't expire on the spot if they had to have a bought loaf now and again or a microwave ready-meal.

The next morning Blossom let Melissa and Greg sleep in— Greg had looked worse than her sister the day before— while she got the children up, gave them their breakfast and took them to nursery. On her way home she visited the local supermarket and bought a load of convenience foods without the merest shred of remorse. Melissa was going to have to lighten up a bit.

As she drew off the road on reaching the house, and into the pebbled front garden which had been given over solely to parking due to the fact that Greg needed a space the size of a football pitch to park successfully, Blossom saw the silver-grey car parked next to Greg's people-carrier and groaned softly. Zak Hamilton. Damn it. And she was in her oldest jeans and a cotton jumper that had been washed so often and become so baggy it could pass for a dress. But she *had* taken the time to apply some mascara that morning and curl the ends of her hair, so that the bob just skimmed her shoulders, having known she was calling in at the supermarket. Overall it was an improvement on the last time they'd met. Not a big one, but something at least. Not that it bothered her what Zak Hamilton thought of her. Not in the least. Not for a second. The very idea!

Ignoring the little voice in the back of her mind that was saying nastily, 'And pigs fly,' she parked the car and began to lift the bags of shopping out. Along with the little voice she was determined to pay no heed to, her stomach was fluttering about as though it was host to a flock of butterflies. If butterflies came in flocks? She wasn't sure about that.

'Hi again.' The deep, faintly accented voice was behind her.

She straightened up so quickly she heard her neck snap, but it was more the fact that she caught a carrier bag on something sharp in the boot, tearing it so that a can of baked beans dropped on her foot, that brought forth the exclamation of pain. Turning, she saw Zak Hamilton walking towards her.

'Want some help with all that?' he offered, waving a hand at the bags round her feet. 'You look pretty loaded up.'

She would have liked to say no, but as she wasn't an octopus it would have been rather silly. She forced a smile, wondering if her toe was broken. 'Thank you,' she said politely.

'You're very welcome.'

As he bent and picked up several of the bags, she caught a whiff of a deliciously sexy and definitely very expensive aftershave. The torn carrier-bag chose that moment to empty itself completely, and in the ensuing scramble for tins and packets of this and that Blossom got control of her breathing. Until she registered Zak crouching down, trousers pulled tight over muscled thighs as he stuffed some of the food into another bag. He was more sexy than any man had the right to be.

'I thought Melissa cooked everything from scratch.' He glanced up at her, a packet of cherry bakewells in his hand, and his eyes so piercingly blue their brightness made Blossom blink.

'She does,' Blossom said shortly, wishing he would stand up. When he obliged in the next instant she felt sufficiently in control again to add, 'But I'm in charge for the next few days until she's feeling a bit better.'

'Ah.' He nodded. 'I wonder if they'll get the kids back to the healthy option once they've tasted fish fingers and oven chips.' He grinned at her, eyebrows raised. 'What do you think?'

'The odd meal like that does no harm at all.' Even to herself she sounded schoolmarmish. 'They're quite nutritious.'

'You know that and I know that, but mother love is a strange force,' he said gravely.

He was laughing at her—again. The difference was this time she found she was having a job not to smile. 'I wouldn't know. I'm just the aunty.' Picking up two bags of her own, she made for the house. There was safety in numbers.

Melissa and Greg were in the sitting room, a tray of coffee and a plate of shortbread fingers on the low oak coffee-table in front of them. Blossom paused at the open door long enough to say, 'I'm just putting the shopping away,' before continuing to the kitchen. A cosy foursome? Not on your life.

'I think I got them out of bed.'

Zak had followed her, and now he dumped his bags on the

breakfast bar as she glanced his way. 'It's half-past ten, don't worry about it,' she said briefly. 'They'd slept enough.'

'Greg made the coffee.' It was faintly plaintive.

There was a message in there somehow, and Blossom raised her eyebrows enquiringly even as she wondered what it was about raven-haired men and pale blue shirts. Killer combination.

'It's as weak as dishwater.' Zak's eyes were laughing at her.

'Oh dear.' That'd teach him to call without warning. 'I'll put the shopping away and make some more; the other is probably cold by now, anyway.' *I'm putting shopping away— hint, hint.*

He nodded. 'Want some help?'

Even standing six feet away he was too close for comfort. Not that she thought he was going to try anything. He was far too sophisticated for anything so gauche and clumsy, she knew that. 'No thanks. I won't be long.' *Just go before I drop something else. Give me a few minutes to do some deep- breathing exercises.*

He didn't take the hint. Folding his arms, he leant back against the open door and watched her. It was disconcerting to say the least. Having grown up with someone as totally stunning as Melissa, she had never liked being stared at, always assuming she was being compared unfavourably to her twin. Maybe that was why she'd chosen a career behind the camera? Interesting thought, she told herself feverishly. Freud would probably have had the time of his life messing with her head. If he hadn't been dead for eight decades, that was.

The shopping disposed of in record time—she'd never be able to find anything now—Blossom switched the kettle on and steeled herself to smile and glance at Zak as she said,

'Shall we join the others? I'll make the excuse about the coffee and bring the tray out.'

'OK.' He made no effort to move. 'Look, I was thinking, with Melissa home after being away so long—' he made five days sound like five lifetimes '—I'd imagine Greg and her would like some time to themselves in the evening once the kids are in bed. And I should think you could do with a change of scene. How about I take you for a meal somewhere tonight? Just as friends, of course. I understand how things are with you.' He smiled lazily as though he didn't care if she came or not.

Blossom stared at him, completely taken aback. 'But we're not friends,' she pointed out gracelessly. 'We don't even know each other, at least not properly. You're just Greg's boss.'

The smile held, but the temperature dropped several degrees. 'I'm not *just* anything,' he said silkily. 'Believe me.'

In spite of the smile Blossom knew she had hit him on the raw. 'I didn't mean—I wasn't insinuating…' She stopped. She had expressed herself incredibly badly. 'I'm sorry,' she said quietly. 'I didn't mean to be rude. It's just that—'

'You don't want to go out with me. Yes, I know. But you must socialise with the male species now and again, surely?'

She was right. She *had* annoyed him. Dented his ego. She imagined Zak Hamilton hadn't been turned down before, even on a friendship level. Well, why would he be?

'Of course, if you feel Melissa's still too ill…'

'No, it's not that.' What was it with him? He had the hide of a rhinoceros. Surely he knew she didn't want to go out—no, *socialise*, she corrected herself with grim humour—with him? But perhaps that was exactly why he was pushing it. Maybe he was one of those men who couldn't resist a challenge. Not that she had intentionally set herself up as a challenge, but she'd bet her last dollar that was how he was viewing this. She didn't buy the 'doing Greg and Melissa a favour' thing, men like Zak weren't that philanthropic. Sharks in disguise.

'So?' Blue eyes held hers. 'What, exactly?'

Oh, blow it, it was going to be easier all around to agree to have a meal with him this evening. She hated that she was going to shy away from further confrontation, but he *was* Greg's boss, and she didn't want to cause waves for her brother-in-law. And that was the only reason she was going to have a meal with him, she reaffirmed firmly to herself. 'I was just thinking of Melissa and Greg,' she lied carefully. 'But I suppose I could see to their meal before you pick me up.'

Zak smiled. 'I'm sure you could, Blossom.'

Blossom wasn't sure about that smile. Was it nice or nasty? A 'great you're coming' smile or a 'knew you'd crumble' one? Either way it was unnerving, to say the least.

'Eight o'clock all right?' he asked easily. 'Enough time to feed and water all your charges?'

'Half-past eight.' She wasn't going to let him think he had it all his own way. Although he had, of course. 'It takes a while to put the children to bed after their meal and bath, and I shall need to see to Melissa and Greg's meal too,' she said primly. 'Melissa is still far from well.'

Zak's mouth twitched. 'Fine,' he said meekly. 'Half-past eight it is. And I promise to not be a second early. OK?'

Wretched man.

The next half hour seemed much longer to Blossom as the four of them sat and chatted over fresh coffee and the shortbread fingers. Although, to be fair, Melissa and Greg didn't touch the shortbread and Zak only had a couple. It was she who had eaten the rest, Blossom thought irritably when Zak stood up to go. It was a failing of hers that she always ate when she was nervous or upset. Comfort thing. And she was doubly nervous at present; Zak's presence in itself was unnerving, but she didn't want him to allude to their meal out together tonight until she'd had a chance to tell Melissa and Greg herself. They knew how she felt about men in general, and non-dating in particular. They'd wonder what on earth was going on if they found out before she could explain properly. If she *could* explain properly. Whatever *properly* was. She didn't think she knew any more. Oh, darn it…

'Thanks for the flowers,' Melissa said to Zak as he made his goodbyes. There was a massive bouquet perched on a chair, waiting for Blossom to see to it. 'And for the champagne.' A bottle of the very best, by the look of it.

'Thought you and Greg might like to celebrate your home-coming,' Zak said lazily. He turned to Blossom. 'You could put it on ice before I pick you up tonight.'

'Tonight?' Melissa honed in, looking hard at Blossom.

'Zak's taking me out for a meal tonight.' Blossom's eyes told her twin to leave well alone as she ushered Zak into the hall. A 'you ignore this at your peril' kind of look.

He paused at the front door, his wickedly long black lashes shading the expression in his eyes, so they were unclear as he said, 'I don't think your sister altogether approves of me.'

Considering Melissa and Greg's livelihood was tied up with Zak, Blossom felt she couldn't give an honest answer to that one. Privately she agreed with him. 'Really?' She hoped she looked innocently surprised. 'Why is that?' she asked carefully.

'Just an impression.'

He didn't sound as if he was bothered, but then why would

he be? He was holding all the cards. 'I'm sure that's not the case,' she said briskly, opening the door. 'See you later, then.'

He pulled out a pair of expensive sunglasses and stepped into the bright July sunlight, walking to the car and sliding into the luxurious interior without glancing behind him. This time she watched him leave, raising her hand when he waved at her. She stood for some moments after the sound of the engine had faded away, her head whirling. Somehow she had promised to go out with Zak Hamilton tonight. It would have seemed an impossibility when she had woken up that morning, but it had happened. This was not good. This was *so* not good.

A movement behind her brought her head turning to Melissa, who was standing in the sitting-room doorway, a worried expression on her face. 'Tell me to mind my own business if you want, but I don't like the idea of you seeing Zak,' her sister said, straight to the point as always. 'He's not for you, Blossom.'

Blossom shut the front door. 'It's not like you think.'

'Blossom, the man's a dyed-in-the-wool bachelor with a different woman for each day of the week. He makes no secret of it. In fact, according to the grapevine, he makes a point of spelling it out to any woman he sees so they don't get the wrong idea. Of course, most of them fall for him hook, line and sinker nonetheless.' Melissa's tone was scathing.

'Melissa, this really isn't what you're thinking.'

'He could charm the birds out of the trees, I've seen him in action, but Greg says he can be as hard as iron in business when it's necessary. And if he can be like that in business...'

'Come and sit down and let me explain,' Blossom said patiently, taking her sister's arm and leading her to the sofa beside Greg. 'You've got the wrong idea.'

'Greg thinks I've got a down on Zak, but it's not that, not really,' Melissa began again before Blossom had a chance to say more. 'It's just that men like him eat ordinary people up and spit them out for breakfast. Greg's useful to him at the moment, but I keep telling him that if that changed he'd be out on his ear and Zak wouldn't give it a second thought.'

'Melissa, I'm not saying I think you're wrong—just the opposite, in fact.' Blossom jumped in when her sister paused for breath. 'But this meal tonight is not a date, not in the traditional sense. It's purely platonic, I assure you.'

'Oh, Blossom, don't be so naïve.'

'No, I mean it. Really. He actually said he wanted to give you and Greg an evening to yourselves and that he was taking me out purely as a friend. OK? He said that.'

'And you believed it? Kiddo, it's the oldest line in the book when a wolf sees a juicy little lamb.'

'I'm not a juicy little anything.' She didn't think she'd ever been juicy, even before Dean. 'And I'm hardly what you'd call his type anyway. I'm sure he goes for long-legged model types with interesting cheekbones and a clothing allowance to die for. Am I right, Greg?' She glanced at her brother-in-law, but didn't wait for him to reply before she went on, 'Anyway, I told him I am not dating. I laid it absolutely on the line. My career's all that matters, he knows that.'

'Then how come you're going out with him tonight?' Melissa asked reasonably. 'The two things don't add up, sis.'

'I told you, it's purely platonic.'

Melissa gave one of her snorts. They were legendary within the family, and had always said far more than words could express.

'It *is*, believe me.' Blossom was getting exasperated.

'I believe you might think so, but you're wrong, Blossom. The man's a walking sex machine; you only have to look at him to see that. He can cause the juices to flow without even trying.'

'*Melissa!*' Greg was shocked.

'Oh, I don't mean I'm attracted to him,' Melissa said quickly. 'I love *you*, you know that, but I have got eyes in my head, Greg, and your boss is…well…'

'She means unattached women would find him drop-dead gorgeous,' Blossom said drily when her sister ran out of words.

'There, you see, you do fancy him,' Melissa said triumphantly. 'And you mustn't, Blossom. This going out with him is a bad idea.'

'You've been telling me for the last couple of years that I *should* date again,' Blossom pointed out. In fact, her sister had waxed lyrical on the subject until they'd nearly fallen out about it and had had to agree to disagree. And not so long ago, either.

'*Date*, yes, even get involved if the man in question is right for you, but Zak Hamilton… I can't think of anyone worse. He's too…too much of everything.'

They agreed on that at least, then. 'Melissa, I have no intention of seeing Zak again after tonight,' Blossom said very firmly. 'I promise, OK? This was just the easy way out tonight. He wouldn't take no for an answer, and I couldn't be bothered to argue. It was simpler all round to say yes.'

Melissa stared unhappily at her twin. 'I don't like it.'

'I mean it. I don't like him, to be honest. He's too…' Blossom couldn't find the words to describe Zak Hamilton. 'Too much of everything, like you said,' she finished weakly.

'I just don't want you hurt again, that's all,' Melissa said woefully. 'You're not a toughie like his other women.'

'I'm not keen on the idea myself.'

'And, you're right, I *do* think you ought to start dating. There are lots of lovely men out there who would give their eye teeth to have someone like you,' Melissa said earnestly. 'Men like Greg, who are gorgeous but still real family-men and completely faithful to one woman. Good, honest, reliable men.'

Greg preened.

Blossom didn't like to point out that, perfect though Greg was for her twin, he would drive her mad after ten minutes. Instead, she smiled, saying, 'We've done this one to death before, sis. And you're looking tired; I think you ought to go for a nap. You don't want to overdo it now you're back home.'

Greg was instantly all concern as Blossom had known he would be. Between them they managed to persuade Melissa to go and lie down, and Greg led her sister out of the room as though any sudden movement would cause her to break.

Blossom carried the coffee cups through to the kitchen, but instead of loading the dishwasher she stood gazing idly at the blue sky dotted with cotton-wool clouds. In truth the conversation with Melissa had unnerved her more than a little. It *was* stupid to go out with Zak Hamilton tonight, be it on a friendship basis or whatever else. A bit like sticking your head in the jaws of a crocodile and not expecting it to do what crocodiles did.

She made a sound of deep irritation in her throat. She wasn't going to think about all this right now. She was going to fetch her nieces and nephew from nursery once she'd finished the chores here and then fix lunch for everyone. This afternoon she would take the children to the nearby water-park. She'd keep busy and active and not allow herself to dwell on the evening ahead for one moment. And when it came she'd play it by ear. She was getting this all out of proportion, for goodness' sake. The man had asked her out for a meal, no strings attached, no expectations. And after tonight she'd probably never run into him again.

'No probably about it.' She watched a tiny blue-tit hanging from a nut holder. He was having the most marvelous time. 'I'll make sure of it.'

Why was she standing here talking to herself? Tut-tutting again, she loaded the dishwasher, cleaned the kitchen floor, did a couple of other chores, and then picked up the car keys from the coffee table and went to fetch the children.

CHAPTER THREE

'SO WHAT are you going to wear?'

The children had been fed, read to and were now fast asleep. The stuffed shoulder of lamb Blossom had bought ready-prepared earlier that day was cooking gently in the oven, and Greg had instructions when to put the roasted vegetables in to join it. She had bought a raspberry trifle for pudding, so that was simple enough. Having bathed, and with her wet hair turban-style in a handtowel, Blossom was standing looking at her meagre wardrobe when Melissa drifted into the room.

'I thought you were sitting having a glass of wine before dinner!' Blossom accused. 'Relaxing with your husband?'

'I was. I shall be again soon. So, what are you going to wear tonight?' Melissa repeated.

'There's not a lot of choice.' When Greg had called to say Melissa had been rushed into hospital, Blossom had grabbed whatever was handy and stuffed it willy-nilly into a suitcase. 'I only brought two dresses with me. I've got jeans and shorts and T-shirts, of course. And a pair of trousers I bought last year.'

Melissa dismissed these with a wave of her hand. 'I like

that dress,' she said, pointing to a cream-and-caramel flowered frock with spaghetti straps. 'Those colours look good on you.'

The dress was fine, but she hadn't brought anything to go with it, and although it was July the evenings could still turn chilly when the sun went down. When she voiced this, though, Melissa's eyes lit up. 'Wait there.' She was back in two minutes, holding a cream ruche-cashmere cardigan and a pair of high wedge-heeled mules in the same colour. 'Bought these a couple of weeks ago to go with a pink dress I'm wearing for a wedding next month,' she said happily. 'You can borrow my diamond bracelet and studs, too, they'd look perfect with this.'

'I can't wear these when you haven't even worn them yet,' Blossom protested. 'What if I spill something down the cardy?'

'When you've been an absolute angel, shooting down here and looking after everyone for days on end? I think so,' Melissa said firmly. 'Ooh, and I've some gorgeous nail varnish, "opal fire", to set those mules off. Twinkling toes and all that.'

'Melissa, this isn't a date.' If she had been feeling panicky before her sister had come in, she felt a hundred times worse now.

'I know, I know,' Melissa said soothingly. 'But you can't go out with a man like Zak and look anything less than perfectly turned out. Not with the sort of women he's seen with.'

Funny, but that didn't help.

At eight-twenty-five Blossom was ready. She had sent Melissa downstairs a long time before this; her sister had been in danger of reducing her to a gibbering wreck.

Blossom stood staring at herself in the bedroom mirror. She couldn't remember the last time she had taken such trouble with her appearance, but it had been worth it. The divorce had robbed her of her self-confidence so badly she'd only wanted to melt into the woodwork when she'd gone out since then. And that wasn't like her. From a child she had always been the chatty, adventurous one, probably to compensate for not matching up to Melissa in looks, although she hadn't realised this until all the heart searching since Dean had left her. But tonight she didn't look too bad. Pretty good, in fact. Passable, at least.

She made her way carefully downstairs—the mules were really very high—to where Melissa and Greg were sitting. 'The lamb will be ready in another fifteen minutes,' she began.

'Forget the lamb, you look sensational.' Melissa stood up and took her hands. 'Doesn't she, Greg?' she added, turning to her husband. 'Tell her she looks absolutely fabulous.'

'You do, Blossom,' said Greg warmly. 'You'll knock 'em dead.'

Blossom blushed. 'The clothes maketh the woman—'

'Stop it.' Melissa shook her gently. '*You* look beautiful, I mean it. You've never known your own worth, Blossom, that's the trouble, and all that with Dean didn't help. Your hair, your skin, your eyes; I know lots of women who'd kill to look half as good as you. Just believe in yourself a bit more.'

Blossom was saved a reply by the sound of the doorbell. Her stomach did a roller-coaster dive and she felt physically sick. Not the best start to the evening, then. 'I'll get the door and we'll just go.' She could not endure the four of them making small talk for five minutes; it was beyond her.

Melissa and Greg had followed her into the hall when she opened the door, as though they were parents inspecting a virgin daughter's first boyfriend. She'd never felt so embarrassed.

'Hi.' Zak expressed no surprise in seeing half the house lined up in the hall. He smiled at Blossom and raised a lazy hand to Greg and Melissa. 'All ready?' he asked as his eyes returned to her. 'The table's booked for nine.'

She nodded. She didn't speak because she couldn't, her mouth had all dried up. He was wearing a pale salmon-pink shirt and tie and charcoal trousers. He was *gorgeous*. Suddenly Blossom realised how stupid she had been. Why on earth had she been thinking Zak Hamilton had offered to take her out for any other reason than to give Greg's sister-in-law a break from the domestic routine? She wasn't a challenge, for goodness' sake. This man didn't need challenges.

It ought to have been reassuring and a relief. Strangely it was merely acutely depressing. Stitching a bright smile on her face, Blossom turned to Melissa and Greg, her goodbye as light as if she didn't have a care in the world.

Zak put his hand on the small of her back as they walked to the Aston Martin. It was a casual gesture, nothing more, but she felt the contact burn her skin through her thin dress.

He opened the passenger door for her and then shut it once she was in her seat. The good manners had the ring of naturalness about them. She watched him as he walked round the gleaming bonnet of the car, and every nerve in her body responded as he slid into the driving seat, glancing at her and smiling as he said. 'Safety belt on, please.'

She obeyed automatically. She fancied him. She fancied him *rotten*. It was a relief to admit it at last. The relief was short lived. In the next breath the realisation that she couldn't have been attracted to a more wildly unsuitable man if she'd tried swept over her. She'd gone down the route of falling head over heels for a handsome, charismatic swine and look where it had got her. Not that Zak would be interested in her money—if she had any, which she didn't. When Dean had cleared her out, she'd gone through a 'hey ho, what's the point in saving a bean when shopping is such good therapy?'

stage. It had stuck. And of course she'd had to change the sofa and curtains and carpets in the flat to make it look different and avoid bad memories.

Her galloping train of thought came to an abrupt halt when Zak reached behind him and brought out a little box, placing it in her lap. 'What's that?' She stared at it as though it was going to bite her.

'Open it and see,' he said reasonably.

Gingerly, her fingers shaking just the slightest, Blossom flicked open the lid. The tiny corsage consisted of two fresh cream rosebuds with just the faintest touch of lemon running through them, secured with strands of fragile fern on a pin. Only the pin wasn't just a pin, she thought, the colour in her cheeks deepening. It was a brooch with a beautifully worked little bee in crystal and silver. At least she hoped it was crystal. The body couldn't be a diamond, could it? Not *that* size. If so, she couldn't possibly accept it. Perhaps she shouldn't accept it anyway. What did one do in these circumstances?

'It reminded me of the story you told me about your and Melissa's names,' Zak said quietly at her side. 'Apt, eh?'

She raised her eyes to his. 'It's beautiful, exquisite, but I can't possibly accept this.' Her cheeks were on fire.

'A corsage?' he said offhandedly as though she was being ridiculous. 'I really don't see why not.'

'But it's not just a corsage.' Her finger moved over the tiny brooch. 'It's more than that, you know it is.'

'Essentially, certainly for tonight, it's a corsage, and when the rosebuds die you will still have something to remember your time here by. A reminder that Melissa recovered, if you like.'

Put like that, it seemed the height of boorishness to

refuse. 'Thank you, it's exquisite,' she said again, and then froze as his hands reached for the corsage which he fastened on to her dress, his fingers not transgressing by so much as an inch.

He was so close the faint tang of that delicious aftershave she had smelt once before teased her nostrils, his tanned skin and jet-black hair filling her vision. And then he leant back into his seat again, and as the world slowly righted itself she started breathing once more. Shakily.

Should she have accepted the corsage in view of the brooch? She wasn't sure. Perhaps he always gave a date something like this. But then, she wasn't a date. Oh, heavens… She glanced down at the rosebuds and the little bee shone back at her. For all she knew he had a girlfriend anyway, but somehow she didn't think so. Not that that mattered to her one way or the other, of course. He could have a dozen—no business of hers.

She breathed in very deeply, collecting her racing thoughts. It had been the right thing to make light of the brooch; to do anything else would have been insulting. She couldn't have refused it. It would have made him feel awkward at the very least.

She glanced at him under her eyelashes as he started the car. Zak didn't look like the type of man who would allow himself to feel awkward, admittedly.

He executed a neat manoeuvre into the road—an exercise which would have baffled Greg—and they were on their way. Blossom felt as though her bottom was skimming the road, the car sat so low, but it was exhilarating, especially because the interior of the car dripped luxury and the powerful engine just purred along. Zak's hands on the steering wheel caught her attention. They were big, long fingered and looked very capable, the sort of hands that would always know exactly what they were doing—whether it was driving this animal of a machine or making love to a woman. Making love…

She caught the thought, turning scarlet and jerking her head to look out of the side window. No more going down that route, she told herself feverishly. What was the matter with her?

'We're going to a little place I know by the river, it's perfect on a night like this,' Zak said lazily. 'It necessitates a bit of a drive, but I'm not familiar with restaurants round Greg's neck of the woods so I thought it safer on the whole. OK with that?'

'Yes, fine, of course.' *Don't babble.* The sort of women he dated would never babble. Taking a deep breath, she said steadily, 'It was kind of you to come all this way to bring Melissa flowers and champagne.' Well, it had been.

'It's no distance with a car like this, if you pick the right time and let the rush-hour subside.' The blue gaze flashed over her face before returning to the windscreen. 'Besides, like I said, I thought you could do with a break from domestic bliss.'

What did that mean—that he had thought of the flowers and champagne first, or seeing her again first?

'Of course, I wouldn't make the effort with all my employees, but I like to think Greg is more a friend than someone who works for me, and I know how cut up he was about Melissa at first. It helped a lot, you coming to hold the fort.'

That was her answer, then. It was the regard with which he held Greg that had brought him. Which was fine, just fine. 'She's my sister, I'd do anything for her. You know how it is.'

'Not exactly. I'm an only child, and my parents divorced when I was a couple of years old.'

'Oh, right. Well, I didn't necessarily mean a brother or sister, just family as a whole. Blood's thicker than water, and all that,' she said quickly, her senses detecting a note in his voice she couldn't quite discern but which disturbed her.

'Again, I wouldn't know. When my mother went off to Texas with the guy she left my father for—he was American, obviously—she took me with her, but I saw more of the domestic help than I did of them. Family life wasn't an option.'

He had spoken quietly and evenly, and without the faintest shred of bitterness, but perhaps it was the complete lack of expression which made her think he wasn't as detached as he seemed. Carefully, she said, 'And your father? Didn't he try to see you?'

'I was shunted over to England several times a year, ostensibly to stay with him. It was part of the divorce agreement, which had been acrimonious to say the least. But I think he only insisted on it to annoy my mother. Each time I arrived I was passed round different relatives—the two sets of grandparents, aunts and uncles, that sort of thing. I was lucky if he made an appearance for more than a day or so. I was a reminder of the big mistake he had made in marrying my mother, you see. And of course I didn't really know any of the family or they me. I was just a weird little American kid who preferred waffles for breakfast rather than cornflakes, and baseball to football.'

She had wondered where the faint accent she detected in his voice had come from. 'You don't sound very American,' she said tentatively, wondering if she was saying the right thing.

'No? Probably because when my mother died when I was ten years old I was shipped back to England and promptly put in boarding school. Then it was university, followed by the big wide world and a series of jobs between which I bummed around Europe. That wasn't a bad time, on the whole. Informative, anyway.'

'You didn't want to work for your father?'

They had just reached a set of traffic lights and now he turned to her, his eyes very blue. 'My father wasn't into the father-and-son thing. He preferred to forget he'd got a son most of the time. I didn't argue with that. It would have been pointless, a waste of my energy and emotion, and I don't like waste.'

Wow. She could see where the ruthlessness Melissa had spoken of came in now. He was scary. She wondered why his father had left Zak the business if they had been estranged when he'd died, but knew she couldn't ask. Instead she said, 'Do you have contact with anyone in the family now?'

The traffic lights changed to green and the powerful car leapt forward. 'No,' said Zak quietly. 'Both sets of grandparents are dead, and I'm not interested in the rest.'

Right. Autonomous, then.

Zak switched the car's CD player on and music filled the brief pause. 'What do you like?' he asked, his eyes on the road. 'Blues, rock, jazz?'

Clearly the end of that brief glimpse into his life. 'Anything and everything, except heavy metal. This is fine.'

His background explained a lot. As they drove on, Blossom started dissecting their conversation. The reluctance to get involved with any one woman for long, the self-governing, independent lifestyle, the air of detachment that hung about him and made him more attractive if anything. Being treated like that as a child by the very people who should have loved and protected him must have been terrible.

Then she caught her errant thoughts. Hang on, he might have been like that anyway, she warned herself silently. It might not be a case of little boy lost who needed a good woman to change his life, but more one of plain old-fashioned genes. And he *was* incredibly handsome, wealthy, successful and intelligent. That combination would be enough to prompt any man's ego to get out of control, and once that happened it was emotional suicide for anyone foolish enough to care about them.

'Your turn to tell me about you.'

His voice had been soft, but it still brought Blossom up straighter in her seat. Help. Did she tell him she wasn't prepared to discuss her past? But how could she? And what if he got the hump and turned the car around and took her back to Melissa's? She wouldn't find out another thing about him then, and she was surprised how he'd whetted her curiosity with what he'd revealed so far.

Curiosity killed the cat. The warning was as clear as if someone had spoken it. *Don't even think about going there.*

Yeah. She gave a mental nod of acknowledgement. Crazy to mess with this man. Even crazier to have agreed to come out with him tonight. Especially as she fancied him without liking him. She'd never been in this position with anyone else. Before Dean she had been quite cautious about her boyfriends, and definitely the liking thing had had to be in place before she'd allowed herself to be attracted physically. With Dean she'd literally been swept off her feet, and it had been tinsel and stardust, and riding off into the sunset together. It wasn't until he'd left she'd realised she hadn't known the real Dean at all, just a romantic image he'd projected to entangle her.

'Blossom? It can't be that complicated, surely?' His voice, teasing now, brought her out of her reverie. 'Start with you and Melissa as little girls growing up and go on from there. Was it a happy childhood?'

'Tremendously so.' She wondered how long she could spin out the time of pigtails and gymslips. Long enough for them to reach the restaurant, perhaps?

She tried to focus her gaze on anything but his hard thighs and the way his trousers stretched over a certain part of his anatomy as she spoke. She made a meal of her time at university and then the battle to get noticed in the career she'd chosen once she'd finished the childhood years.

Zak said very little, interjecting the odd question now and again but letting her ramble on. She kept her conversation light and entertaining, focusing on her work and the goings-on in the fashion world, and feeling a sense of accomplishment all out of proportion to the deed when she succeeded in making him chuckle once or twice. His sense of humour was very like hers. After all, she told herself reassuringly, Zak had not mentioned anything about his love life, so why should she go down that path? And to be fair he probably hadn't even expected her to. She was super-sensitive about what had happened with Dean, she knew that. Prickly even. And long after the hurt and pain had vanished the feeling of intense humiliation had remained.

They arrived at the river-side pub on the outskirts of London in warm summer twilight, the air hazy and carrying the scent of the myriad window-boxes festooning the building. The restaurant was at the back of the pub and was clearly a later addition to the original building, although the 'olde worlde' charm had been maintained. Large French doors opened on to a green sloping lawn which led to the river bank. Lots of couples and families were sitting at the tables and chairs dotting the lawn or lying on the grass, and the scene was a relaxing and lazy one. Very English, very normal.

Blossom felt out of sync with the rest of the world, being anything but relaxed as she gazed out of the doors from the small table for two where she and Zak had been seated. When they had left the car he'd done the hand-on-the-small-of-her-back thing again and she knew her cheeks were still burning. Which was absurd, and so gauche of her. It wasn't as if she did breathless and blushing, she never had.

'Can I get you a drink while you look at the menu?' A smiling waitress who was all pert breasts and fluttering lashes and couldn't have been a day older than eighteen was busy giving Zak the eye as she spoke.

He didn't seem to be aware of it, to be fair. His eyes on Blossom, he said, 'Shall we toast Melissa's recovery with a bottle of champagne, considering they're probably doing the same thing at this moment?'

'Lovely.' She would actually have preferred a glass of still wine—she had always found champagne a little dry for her taste—but she didn't like to say so with Little Miss Come-and-get-me standing there. She felt awkward enough as it was.

Once the waitress had disappeared, Blossom quickly buried her head in the huge embossed menu. She had already worked out this was not your average pub, and the vast choice of superb meals on offer, not to mention the prices, confirmed this. She had always been a girl who lived to eat, unlike Melissa who ate to live—hence her sister's sylph-like shape and her own more generous curves, Blossom thought ruefully. Now the fabulous array of perfectly delicious-sounding options made her mouth water despite her nerves.

'Can I suggest the truffled salad of confit spring-chicken with chicory, scallions and pancetta to begin with?' Zak murmured after Blossom had scanned the menu umpteen times without coming to a decision and had become thoroughly confused.

She lowered the menu and looked at him. The piercing blueness of his eyes took her breath away. How did other women feel when they woke up beside a man like this? She'd felt inadequate with Dean, always trying to slip out of bed before he was awake to at least brush her teeth, get some mascara on and do something with her hair. She had felt she needed to try all the time. Perhaps that should have told her something, in hindsight? Yes, if she thought about it, it definitely should have. She'd never felt quite good enough for Dean, and it had been he who had made her feel that way. She just hadn't realised it at the time. She had blamed it all on herself.

'The chicken?' she repeated a little vaguely before pulling herself together. 'Yes, that sounds great.' She smiled her first natural smile of the evening. 'I'm afraid looking at all these fantastic dishes has blown my mind. I'm bad enough at deciding if there's just three or four options, let alone a dozen and more for each course. And they all look so delicious.'

He grinned. It increased the sex appeal by about one hundred per cent. 'In that case, the grapefruit-and-mango sorbet to follow clears the palate wonderfully for the roast rib of beef with kumquats, or perhaps you'd prefer the organic salmon with cannelloni beans? I've had both and can recommend either.'

'The beef sounds delicious.' Who'd been with him those other times?

'It is, trust me.'

Looking like you do? Never. Blossom nodded. 'The beef it is, then. Decision made.' She smiled brightly.

The waitress was back, more goo-goo-eyed than ever.

Blossom found herself focusing on the baby-soft complexion, blonde curls and bright, eager eyes. The girl was little more than a child, and yet clearly possessed of a self-confidence that was daunting. He would have babies like this, full-grown women and perhaps even mature matrons throwing themselves at him all the time. How could one female ever hold the attention of a man like him? She'd have to be nothing short of Aphrodite.

The champagne wasn't the fizzy, dry, somewhat acidic stuff Blossom had had in the past, but a mellow, effervescent wine that sat on the tongue presenting strawberries and honey and the essence of summer days. She didn't like to think what it had cost, but it certainly wasn't your average common-or-garden variety. Now she understood why some of the top models she worked with drank champagne and nothing else. Of course they were also aware that champagne, unlike all other alcoholic beverages, didn't put any weight on. A big plus in the world of stick insects they inhabited, she thought wryly.

'So…' As though she had just finished talking a moment ago, Zak said, 'You and Melissa lost your parents four years ago. Any other close relatives?'

'Not what I'd call close, as such. We tend to get together with various aunties and uncles and cousins at weddings and funerals and special occasions and such like. My mother's parents died some time ago, but my father's are still alive and living in New Zealand. They emigrated just before Melissa and I were born and we've only seen them a few times. We don't really know them.'

'But you and Melissa have each other.'

'Yes, we do. And Melissa has Greg and the children, of course, and she's very generous about including me in things.'

He nodded thoughtfully. 'And you've never been tempted to follow her example after seeing such domestic bliss—go down the normal route in life?'

'Normal?' Blossom's laughter was hollow. 'What's normal?'

He surveyed her lazily, his voice smoky soft when he said, 'Most ladies of my acquaintance want a partner, children, the nest thing. Even the most severely career-minded tend to have some in-built biological clock that starts ringing eventually. I lost a couple of damn good secretaries that way,' he added as an afterthought, frowning.

'You ought to inhabit the fashion and modelling world.' Blossom grimaced. 'Believe me, roses round the door and bonny, bouncing babies aren't a priority with girls terrified they might put on an extra pound if they eat a chocolate bar or whatever.'

'Good tip. I'll look for a secretary there next time one skedaddles.' He flexed his shoulders, taking a sip of his champagne before he said, 'But you aren't a model, you're a photographer. Behind the camera. So, the question still holds.' He smiled easily but his gaze was hard on her face.

'What question?' She was playing for time and she knew it, which in the circumstances was futile. Zak wouldn't give up.

'The roses round the door and bonny, bouncing babies thing—it holds no appeal whatsoever? Not in a few years, perhaps?'

She stared at him. If she was to answer truthfully it would be to say that up until the day Dean had left her she had never imagined she wouldn't have a family one day in the future. She hadn't been in a hurry when she'd met him, but neither had she thought she'd go through life childless. Now…

'Let's just say any appeal is far outweighed by remaining focused on what I really want,' she prevaricated carefully.

The tendency to glance into pushchairs these days, the odd sojourn into baby boutiques even when she wasn't looking for presents for her nephew and nieces, the painful darts in her heart region, certain advertisements featuring women with full, rounded bellies or new mothers holding dimpled sleeping, infants brought forth—

All that was *her* business. Something she hadn't shared with anyone.

'A woman who really knows her own mind.' He smiled. 'And you've clearly got the drive and determination to make what you want happen. I'm impressed, Blossom.'

He didn't look impressed, somehow. She couldn't quite pin down the shadowed look in his eyes but it belied the smile. 'Good.' It was cool and dismissive, and she fully intended it to sound that way. He was the one who had forced her to say what she had, after all. If he disapproved for some reason, tough. She wasn't about to answer to Zak Hamilton for anything.

'And so you don't have fun, don't date, don't let your hair down, *ever*? It's all work, work, work?'

If the champagne hadn't been so delicious she would have thrown it over him. It was for all the world as though she had just confessed to being an axe murderer. 'Of course I have fun,' she said stiffly. 'That doesn't necessarily have to go hand in hand with dating or having a man in my life. Believe it or not, the male sex is not the be all and end all of life. Women can get by without you, impossible though that sounds.'

'I'm wounded.' He grinned. 'And I trust that "you" wasn't meant for me personally?'

Blossom shrugged, refusing to melt. Having a conversation with Zak Hamilton was like the Spanish Inquisition. 'Frankly,' she said primly, 'I don't think there's anything wrong in this day and age with being celibate, if you want to know. I know too many girls who wake up the next morning not knowing who they've gone to bed with the night before.'

Zak's mouth twitched. 'I promise you that when I take you into my bed you'll remember every moment the next morning in vivid detail. How about that?' The gaze was wicked.

'Your confit spring-chicken?'

The waitress had returned with their first course, her sparkling eyes alight with a mixture of delight and envy. She had clearly heard every word. Blossom's face matched the single scarlet rose in the bud vase in the centre of the table. She gulped at her champagne until the girl had gone, then bit back the hot words hovering on her tongue. She was not going to give even a hint of credibility to that remark by stating she had no intention of ever gracing his bed.

Zak didn't seem bothered one way or the other, waving his fork at her as he said, 'This is delicious, as good as I remember. Try some. I guarantee you'll love it.'

She would have *loved* to lean across and tip the contents of the whole table into his lap, then leave with her nose in the air. The resulting mess and clatter would be wonderfully satisfying. But it was a long way back to Melissa's, and the food *did* look exceptionally good. And she felt hungry.

She watched him as he lifted the champagne bottle from its icy bucket and refilled her glass to the brim, before adding just a smidgen to his own. 'Driving,' he said in answer to her unspoken question. 'I only ever have one glass when I'm driving.'

Model citizen. Blossom's lip curled. Then she picked up her knife and fork and began to eat.

CHAPTER FOUR

THE meal was wonderful, and when Zak suggested cherrimisu for dessert—a delicious chocolate-and-cherry dish somewhere between a Black Forest gateau and a tiramisu—Blossom didn't protest, even though she was full. She'd diet it away tomorrow.

Zak had been a perfect gentleman since the bed remark, his conversation light and entertaining, and his body language easy and non-threatening. Somewhere between the sorbet and the beef Blossom found herself relaxing and enjoying the evening, helped not a little by several glasses of champagne. It wasn't until she rose to her feet once she had finished the cherrimisu and before coffee was served that she realised the wine was really very potent. And she had drunk four glasses to Zak's one. A ploy on his part, with the drive home in mind?

She tottered into the ladies' cloakroom on Melissa's high wedges and breathed a sigh of relief once she was safely in and the door to the restaurant was closed. She glanced at her reflection in the long mirror over the neat row of shining washbasins. Wide, bright eyes stared back at her along with cheeks dusted with pink. The face was that of a woman who had been enjoying herself. More than that, the eyes had a starry quality to them and her smile was slightly flirtatious.

Blossom straightened her mouth at once, frowning. She dabbed cold water over her wrists and pulled a brush through her thick, silky hair although it hadn't needed it.

No more champagne and lots of coffee. She nodded to the thought. She dared bet he would make a pass at her at some point on the way home, and she wanted to be absolutely compos mentis when she rebuffed him. No hesitation, no vacillation; that wouldn't do with a man like Zak Hamilton. Any weakness on her part and he would pounce for the kill. And she didn't flatter herself that he particularly fancied her either. As she had originally suspected, she was now sure he saw her merely as a challenge, nothing more. She would be the world's biggest fool to be tempted, and she had had enough of playing that no-win role. Nowadays *she* was in control of her emotions. Always.

Zak was leaning lazily back in his chair when she walked into the restaurant, idly glancing around him. Blossom paused for some moments in the doorway, watching him. Or, rather, watching people watching Zak. Women, to be precise. He was receiving the same covert glances, the same interest, that Dean had when they had been out in a public place.

Her eyes lingered on a pretty redhead who seemed unable to tear her eyes away from Zak. The redhead's companion looked to be a nice man, good looking in a sort of stout, tweeds-and-pipe, pillar-of-the-community way. Blossom could tell the man had noticed the redhead's interest but was trying to ignore it. She didn't understand women like this one, although she had come into contact with quite a few in the months she had been with Dean. Women who made it clear they were available even though they were with someone else. It was so rude for everyone concerned.

She marched across the room and took her seat, turning and looking the other woman straight in the eye after she had sat down. The redhead's green gaze narrowed before lowering to the food in front of her. Tweeds-and-pipe pretended he hadn't seen.

It was a small victory, silly even. Blossom acknowledged this at the same time as reaffirming she needed the coffee.

'Cream and sugar?' Zak pushed both towards her as she turned to him. 'And there's some home-made chocolates, too.'

Gritting her teeth, Blossom said, 'I'll have black, please.' Penitence for the overindulgence with the champagne, because she *hated* black coffee. She also hated lowering herself to the moral standards of the redhead, which was what she felt she'd done in showing the woman her annoyance.

Although, hang on a minute… Blossom drank half the cup of coffee straight down, scalding hot as it was. Why shouldn't she demand some respect? That was all she had been doing.

'Would you like a brandy to go with that?'

She raised her gaze to see Zak's eyebrows quirked enquiringly. In view of her anger at the redhead and Zak—in the latter case unfairly, she admitted, because as far as she could ascertain he hadn't even been aware of the woman's interest—Blossom felt a horribly inappropriate knot of desire somewhere deep in the pit of her stomach as she looked into the sapphire eyes. 'No, thank you,' she said tightly. 'I've had too much champagne as it is.' Just to let him know that she *was* aware of it, and was taking the pertinent action by way of the black coffee.

'OK.' Zak half-smiled and selected one of the chocolates. Blossom sighed inwardly. Here she was turning herself inside out and the swine was so relaxed it wasn't true. It also wasn't fair. But then when was life ever fair? Only in fairy tales. In real life the Juliettes and redheads of this world walked off with the guy every time. Or so it seemed.

'You didn't meet a troll in the ladies' cloakroom, did you?'

'What?' Blossom's gaze focused. What on earth had he said?

'It's just that you've been glaring into thin air since you returned, and I think you might be ruining our fellow diners' appetites. A few of them are looking quite nervous.'

'Very funny.' She couldn't help a slight curve of her lips.

'That's better. Let them enjoy their food.'

Somehow his fingers had reached her hand and were slowly stroking her skin. Blossom tried to ignore what it was doing to her nerve endings. Nerve endings she hadn't known existed in some places. Wondering how she could extract the hand not holding her coffee cup without being too obvious, Blossom said a little croakily, 'I hadn't realised how much champagne I'd had, that's all. I don't like feeling tipsy.'

'Don't worry, you're in safe hands.' His fingers had found the sensitive flesh above her pulse on her wrist.

Ha! The oldest line in the book used by the worst wolves.

'Your skin is like silk,' Zak murmured. 'And your hair has that quality, too. Silky, soft, scented.' His gaze began to wander over her face. 'I want to bury my hands in your hair and draw you close.' He suddenly let go of her and sat back in his seat with something akin to surprise on his face. 'Hell, that sounded like something out of a third-rate movie,' he said with comical chagrin. 'I'm not normally so crass.'

Blossom was glad he didn't know how much he'd affected her. She had been sitting as spellbound as a rabbit before the headlights of an oncoming car. Forcing a smile, she said, 'It can't be the champagne, you've only had one glass. Perhaps you're just losing your touch?'

Something glittered in the blue eyes. 'Is that a challenge?'

Had it been? In her subconscious? 'Of course not.' Blossom gave herself a mental telling-off. She couldn't afford to be like this. Damn the champagne. She must watch herself.

'Pity.' His smile caused her heart to start to pound uncomfortably fast. 'I've always loved a challenge.'

'Well, it wasn't,' she said very firmly, just so he knew.

'OK, I get the message.'

Then why was he still looking so pleased with himself? Blossom buried her nose in her coffee cup, drained it and reached for a refill. Bring on the caffeine, she thought darkly.

'Allow me.' He'd anticipated her, and as their fingers touched on the coffee jug Blossom felt the contact down to her toes. She shakily exhaled. This was crazy, ridiculous. She was thirty-four years old, for goodness' sake, not a fourteen-year-old schoolgirl out on her first date. She'd been married, she knew all there was to know about sex and lust and the rest of it, so how come fireworks went off with just the feel of his hand on hers? That had never happened with Dean, and she'd been head over heels in love then. It was more than disconcerting.

'Thank you.' She lifted the now-full cup of coffee and drank as though she had been in the Sahara without any water for weeks. She'd never felt so out of her depth in all her life as she did right now. The thought of the long drive home in the scented dark night with Zak was making her weak at the knees.

In the event, it was something of an anti-climax. After Zak had paid the bill—giving the blonde waitress an extremely generous tip if her breathless 'Oh, *thank you*, sir,' was anything to go by—they had walked out to the car, but this time his hand on the small of her back was absent. She'd missed the contact. Which warned her yet again she was playing with fire. Not that she didn't already know.

Once she was safely installed in the car he closed the passenger door before walking round the bonnet, his black hair shining in the moonlight. She had a momentary weird feeling that all this was a dream, that she couldn't really be with this gorgeously magnetic man in the sort of car normally only seen on the silver screen. Then he slid in beside her, fastening his seat belt after glancing to see hers was secured, and they were off as the powerful car growled into life. And she knew it wasn't a dream. It was mind-blowing reality.

They didn't chat so much on the way home. Zak seemed a little preoccupied. Now, far from wondering when he was going to make a move on her, Blossom was thinking he couldn't wait to be rid of her. He'd done his duty and taken her out for a meal as a sort of favour to Greg, she thought dismally, and now clearly wanted to get back to his normal life.

When they scrunched into Melissa's front garden Blossom knew she hadn't drunk enough coffee. Why else would she be mourning the fact that she wouldn't know what it was like to be kissed by Zak? Talk about inconsistency.

The house was in darkness except for a dim light showing from the hall through the glass in the front door. 'Looks like everyone's in bed,' Blossom said brightly, just to start the 'thank you for taking me out, and goodbye' speech she'd been rehearsing for the last few miles. Nice and casual and short.

'I've enjoyed tonight.' Zak turned towards her, one arm sliding along the back of her seat. 'Very much.'

She felt the world stop spinning. She wanted to say

something, something light, but nothing came to mind. Not with his arm round her shoulders and the faint tang of that toe-curlingly sexy aftershave in her nostrils. All she could do was watch as his mouth came closer…

The kiss was non-invasive at first, a warm stroking of her lips that was incredibly sweet. Her eyes shut, she drank in the sensations his mouth and his body warmth were creating, a trembling starting somewhere deep in the core of her. How long it was before the kiss deepened she didn't know, but her lips had parted involuntarily to allow him access, and the heady rush of desire that followed took her unawares. Something like an electric shock coursed through her when his tongue fuelled the pleasure, the deep, soft darkness outside the car cocooning them in a world of taste and touch that was breathtakingly erotic. Dangerous, too, but so, so delectable.

She had known he would be good at this, but the little needles of sheer, primitive passion and the sensual stirring of her blood had her quivering in a way she couldn't hide; it was as though she had no control of her body. She was mesmerised, enchanted by what he was doing to her, all reserve abandoned as thrills of excitement trembled down her spine.

'You're beautiful…' The murmur was soft against her skin. 'And potent, like warm wine. If we weren't in a car outside your sister's house…'

The words, quiet and barely a breath in the shadows, were nevertheless enough to break the spell. Her eyes opened to look into his as an awareness of what she was doing hit. The brilliance of the blue eyes, so bright in the darkness, held her still for one more moment and then she pulled away from him, pressing against the passenger door as she whispered, 'I have to go in, I can't do this. I'm sorry, but I just can't.'

'Can't do what?' The murmur was warm, smoky.

'This.' She fumbled for the handle, suddenly desperate to escape. 'I don't want this.'

'A goodnight kiss?' he said lazily, leaning back in his seat.

She didn't answer, half falling out of the car as she heard him swear softly before opening his own door. As she righted herself he reached her, taking her hand when she would have brushed past him. 'What's the matter?' he asked softly. 'Hell, I wasn't about to force you, woman. You were perfectly safe.'

Not from herself. Breathing deeply, Blossom fought for control. 'I'm sorry,' she said as evenly as she could, 'but I don't want to get involved. I mean, I don't want—' She took another breath. 'I don't want to kiss you, I don't want to kiss anyone. I'd made that perfectly clear before tonight.'

'OK, OK, calm down,' he said soothingly.

He was looking at her as though she was mad, and perhaps she was, Blossom thought hysterically. One minute there with him all the way, and the next behaving like an outraged virgin.

'Have you been hurt—physically? Are you afraid of me?'

She groaned inside. This was awful, humiliating. She shook her head wordlessly, not trusting her voice.

He continued to look at her searchingly. 'But I heard fear in your voice,' he said steadily. 'And don't tell me I'm wrong.'

Fear at her own weakness where he was concerned. She had rejected all suitors in the last couple of years or so with very little effort; none of them had even impinged on her consciousness for more than a brief moment. She didn't understand what it was about Zak that changed everything, took away any control over her own reactions, but it frightened her to death. She had been a puppet on a string for one man, and once was enough. 'I told you earlier, I don't date,' she managed at last. 'I don't want any complications in my life, that's all.'

'It was a goodnight kiss,' he repeated softly. 'Nothing more.'

To him, maybe. To her it had been much, much more. A reawakening of the feminine side of her which wanted a life other than that of a solitary bed, and breakfast for one. But she knew she wasn't made for casual affairs or the odd romp in the hay. Some women could give their bodies without their heart being involved, but she couldn't. It was as simple as that. And as she had no intention of giving her heart away again, now she had managed to put the broken pieces back together, that left her no choice but autonomy.

'I'm sorry, Zak.' The whirling frenzy in her head caused by his love-making had cleared, and she saw with absolute clarity she had to end this before it started, certainly in her own mind. Maybe he wouldn't have wanted to see her again— she didn't know for sure—but that had no relevance in any way. 'It was a lovely meal and I've enjoyed the evening, but I have to go.'

'Do I take that as a covert message that you have no wish to repeat the exercise?' His voice was cooler now and his eyes held no warmth.

Blossom looked him straight in the face. 'You knew how it was before this evening,' she said flatly. 'I made it very clear, like I said just now. I don't say one thing and mean another. I—'

'Don't date. Yes, I know.' He paused, running a hand through his hair. 'But isn't that open to compromise? You say you enjoyed this evening. So did I, very much. I would like to repeat it. That's not a crime, is it?'

She said nothing. There was nothing to say, after all.

He waited a moment. 'A career only lasts for so long, Blossom,' he said quietly. 'One day, when you're an old lady and others have taken your place, you'll regret you are on your own with just a cat for company. And it'll be too late then.'

'I'm not over-fond of cats.' Trite, but she couldn't do this, it was killing her. 'Goodbye, Zak.'

'I don't believe I'm getting the full story here.'

She stared at him. Any other man—*any* other man—would have been long since gone after such a rebuff. What was it with him? 'I don't know what you mean,' she prevaricated warily. If he thought she was going to indulge in a heart-on-the-sleeve scenario, he was *so* wrong. All she wanted was for him to go.

'I think you do.' He had moved closer somehow, although he hadn't altered his position by a fraction of an inch. 'Things don't add up with you, Blossom White. There's too many little details that don't fit the image you're trying to project. You're not as tough as you'd like people to believe.'

'I am, actually.' She glared at him to prove the point.

'No.' He shook his head, his eyes glinting in the moonlight. 'I've lived in the world of sharks and barracudas on two legs who would sell their own mother to get up the ladder another inch or two. I can recognize men and women with that ruthless streak a mile off, and you don't have it.'

'You don't know me at all,' she said tightly. 'We've only met a few times. We're virtual strangers.'

'That has nothing to do with it.' He crossed his arms over his chest, his stance suddenly lazy. 'You tell me you are tough, that the only thing that matters is your career and getting it up another notch—right so far?'

'Absolutely.' She hoped her voice didn't betray the trembling inside. She willed herself to stand absolutely still.

'And you have no interest in sharing your life with someone? Of considering a future with a partner, children? Bearing in mind, of course, that that doesn't negate your continuing with your career if you so wish. Millions of women do both.'

She should never have agreed to go out with him tonight. She had known it all along, so she had no excuse for the mess she had made of things. Forcing the shakiness out of her voice, she said clearly, 'No, I've told you. Quite frankly, it's not something I would want to put myself through.' *Let him believe the lie, let me be convincing.* 'I've seen some of those determined career women desperately trying to juggle home commitments, sick children, a husband who begins to resent the fact he's called on to help out more than he thinks he should be. They wear themselves to a frazzle, and nothing is done well in the end. Either that or they have a breakdown eventually, trying to be superwoman. It simply isn't worth it.'

'Now, you see, you tell me that in a very cool and well-thought-out way, but I don't believe you,' he said thoughtfully. 'Why do you think that is?'

'I've no idea.' She stared at him unblinkingly.

He smiled crookedly. 'The hell you haven't,' he said pleasantly. 'I'd give a great deal to read that mind of yours.'

This time she had no warning he was going to kiss her. One moment he was surveying her through reflective moonlit eyes, the next she found herself in his arms and moved into a position where the soft fullness of her breasts was pressed against the hard wall of his chest. His mouth was as intoxicating and knowing as before, but this time the fire was there from the start, giving her no time to marshall her defences. The feel of his body as he held her close heightened what his mouth was doing to her senses, the blood surging through her veins in answer to the sensual assault.

Her heart pounding, she knew she had to object, to pull away, but as each moment intensified the pleasure and delight of being in his arms like this held her captive. Captive and willing.

And then, with an almost cynical command of himself, Zak lifted his head and moved her out of his arms. She stared at him, her heart beating wildly and her cheeks flushed. 'I don't believe you,' he said again, almost coldly, and then turned and walked back to the car.

She turned, fumbling in her bag for her key, and almost falling into the hall once she had opened the front door. Shutting it, she leant against its support on trembling legs, hearing the car engine gradually fade away into the quiet of the night as he drove away.

She stood for some time in the quietness of the house, feeling as though she had just escaped some catastrophic disaster. Let that be a lesson to you, she told herself silently when she finally stopped trembling. Play with matches, and ten to one you'll start a fire, and the normal kind was nothing to the one Zak would be capable of lighting. He was an extraordinary man.

Slowly she made her way to her room, her head whirling and her mind replaying the last few minutes before he had gone. After getting ready for bed, she found sleep was a million miles away, however. Annoyingly she couldn't shut down, even though she felt physically tired. Zak was there, dominating her mind, causing her to go over and over the events of the evening until she felt like screaming at her own weakness.

Annoying man. Irritating man. She turned over in bed, pulling her pillow over her head. But still, quite…extraordinary.

CHAPTER FIVE

'So HOW did the evening go?'

When Blossom came down to breakfast the next morning, having overslept—a result of having lain awake until dawn—it was to see a solitary Melissa at the kitchen table.

'Greg's taken the children to the park,' her sister continued, pouring Blossom a cup of coffee and sliding it towards her as Blossom sat down. 'So we're by ourselves.'

From somewhere in the depths of her Blossom found she could dredge up a smile. From a child her twin had been transparent, and Blossom had no doubt Greg and the children had been despatched out of the way so Melissa could get the full lowdown on her evening with Zak in peace and quiet. But her sister did love her and have her best interests at heart, and she needed to confide in someone this morning, and who better than her twin?

Nevertheless, she took several sips of the scalding hot coffee before she said, 'Depends how you look at it.'

'Oh no.' Melissa's big brown eyes narrowed. 'I knew it. He's charmed you. He has, hasn't he?'

'No. Yes. I mean—' Blossom stopped abruptly. What did

she mean? She was darned if she knew. 'The meal was great, *he* was great, and he wanted to see me again,' she said flatly. 'I said no deal, and we left on…difficult terms.'

'Difficult?' Melissa popped two slices of bread in the toaster and gave Blossom her full attention again. 'Difficult as in embarrassing, or difficult meaning a full-scale row?'

'No, nothing like a row.' Blossom pushed her hair out of her eyes wearily. She'd had about three hours' sleep and she was shattered. 'But embarrassing, yes. For me, anyway. For him it was more a matter of proving a point.'

'Proving a point? I don't understand.' Melissa frowned.

'It's a long story.' And she didn't come out of it well.

'We've got an hour or two.' The toaster pinged, and Melissa buttered the toast and then pushed the plate towards Blossom along with the marmalade and jam pots. Home-made, of course. 'Eat that and then we'll talk. You look awful.'

Frankness was something she could live without today. She ate the toast slowly, but eventually she couldn't prevaricate any longer. She could see Melissa was all agog.

As she put the last morsel in her mouth, Melissa whipped the plate away and leant forward. 'Right, tell me.'

So she did, all of it, including her thoughts and emotions.

When she finished they sat looking at each other in silence for a moment, then Melissa said, 'Oh, Blossom.'

The simple way Melissa had said her name brought a lump to Blossom's throat. 'I know what you're thinking.' Blossom swallowed the lump. 'Headcase.'

'Not a bit of it,' said Melissa indignantly. 'I just wish it was someone more…run of the mill you'd met. Because Zak isn't, is he? Whatever he is, he isn't your average man.'

'No. He isn't,' Blossom agreed ruefully.

'And, even if you were thinking of seeing him again, which you're not, it wouldn't work, would it?'

'No. It wouldn't.'

'This isn't helping much, is it?' Melissa said sadly.

'No. It's not.' They stared at each other miserably.

'I feel awful. You'd never have met him if you hadn't come here to help us out. This is all my fault.'

'Don't be daft.' Blossom gave herself a big mental shake and squeezed her sister's hand. 'Sooner or later it was on the cards I'd meet someone who would…'

'Rattle your cage?' Melissa offered helpfully when she struggled for words.

Blossom didn't know if she liked the 'cage' bit, but she nodded anyway. 'Exactly. And it's actually a positive thing. Now I know I'm not open to persuasion, and it's confirmed everything I'd told myself about remaining single.'

'It has?' said Melissa miserably. 'Oh, don't say that.'

Blossom grinned. She couldn't help it. She knew there was nothing her sister would like more than to be an aunty. 'I don't want a man in my life, I'm perfectly happy as I am.' Her gaze didn't waver as it held Melissa's. 'OK? But there is one thing. And this is important to me. Really important.'

'What?'

'I want you and Greg to promise me you won't say anything about Dean and what happened—me being married, everything—if Zak should ask. I mean I'm not expecting him to,' she added hastily. 'But just in case. It's far better he thinks I'm a dedicated career woman. Which I am,' she said as an afterthought. 'You know that as well as anyone.'

'Of course you are,' Melissa agreed distractedly. 'But what if Greg lets something slip? You know what he's like.'

'Make sure he doesn't,' Blossom said grimly. 'I mean it, sis. Drum it in to him before he goes back to work. I mean it's not as if he's thick or something, just the opposite.'

Melissa nodded unconvincingly. It wasn't reassuring.

'And *if*—and I'm not expecting he will, far from it, like I said before—Zak wants my telephone number or something like that, Greg will have to make some excuse. No, better still, he can say I've made him promise not to give it out.'

'All right.' Melissa sighed deeply. Looking into Blossom's eyes, she said vehemently, 'I never thought I could hate anyone like I hate Dean. I never did like him, you know, but I hate him now.'

'Don't waste your energy. He isn't worth it.' And for the first time since the divorce Blossom realised she meant every word. Dean was history.

Blossom returned to her flat in London five days later, and she hadn't seen hide nor hair of Zak Hamilton in that time. Which was fine. Exactly how she wanted it. She told herself this several times a day once she was home. It was all part of the exercise in purging herself of the self-pity which had crept in after the disastrous evening with Zak.

It didn't matter that she had been the perfectly innocent one in her marriage break-up, who had taken all the hurt and grief, she told herself firmly. The loss of self-confidence, the humiliation, the damage to her self-esteem—she couldn't dwell on those for ever. People suffered much worse and lived to fight another day. As she had.

And, she affirmed over and over again, she had much to be thankful for. Her photography skills were in more demand than ever, she had no financial worries, she was young and healthy and her own person. She was answerable to no one, and that had definite advantages. She could please herself in what she did and when she did it: take the jobs she liked, refuse those she didn't. Travel or stay at home. Be up at the crack of dawn at weekends or stay in bed all day. The list was endless. Positively endless.

After a week she didn't have to repeat the list quite so rigorously before she felt like getting up in the morning. After two weeks she barely went through it at all, and by the time a month had passed she was back to her old self.

Almost. Annoyingly she found, however strong and positive she was in the day, her dreams seemed to have a mind of their own, populated by tall, dark shadows and achingly half-remembered sensations. She was forever chasing something unobtainable in them, searching, reaching out to she knew not what. Or perhaps she did, she thought in her more honest moments. Whatever, she was determined to get the victory of the night hours too. It was just a matter of time. She had thought she would die when Dean had betrayed her, but time had worked a healing she would have thought impossible in the early days.

The middle of August found the country basking in a heatwave. Every lunchtime, and in the humid warm evenings, the London parks were full of folk relishing the hot weather, the exotic smell of suntan lotion competing with the dust and fumes of baking-dry streets. Air conditioning was the new must-have.

It was now five weeks since Blossom had returned to the capital and she had worked like a Trojan every day, including weekends. She told herself it was because she loved her job, and the stimulus it gave her, added to which you were only as good as your last picture, and it didn't do to rest on one's laurels in the fashion world. All of which was perfectly true. What she didn't choose to do was to delve any further into her need for constant activity to fill every waking moment of every day. No more personal witch-hunts for the present.

This particular evening, as she walked the last few yards from the tube to her flat in a large terraced house in Mayfair, she had to admit to herself she was glad it was a Friday night, and that the weekend stretched before her with nothing more important to do than eat and sleep. She hadn't been doing much of either lately, although it hadn't been all bad; she had lost that persistent spare tyre which had been with her since Christmas.

'Hello, Blossom.' The male voice was very deep, and the slight accent carried the husky edge she remembered.

Blossom turned to face Zak slowly; her thought processes seemed to have frozen. The hard-boned face was expressionless and he didn't move from his stance against the wall of a neighbouring house. She realised with a little shock of surprise she must have walked straight past him. 'Hello,' she said at last.

'You're a hard woman to find.' He straightened, his hands in his pockets. 'A regular female Scarlet Pimpernel.'

'I beg your pardon?' She tried to sound disdainful.

'Greg couldn't be persuaded to give me your number, and you're ex-directory. But of course you know that.'

She stared at him. She had gone ex-directory in the aftermath of Dean leaving, when she had reverted to her maiden name. She hadn't wanted any of his friends or colleagues phoning her, and she used her mobile ninety per cent of the time anyway. 'Greg was doing what I asked him to,' she said flatly.

'I know.' He smiled. 'I'm impressed by his loyalty.'

As before he was expensively dressed, but this time in a short-sleeved shirt and casual cotton trousers. The clothes didn't deflect the tangible masculine aura that sat on the big frame one iota. But then nothing could. It was part of him.

Blossom swallowed hard. 'Why are you here, Zak?'

The black brows rose cynically. It was very sexy. 'You know why I'm here, Blossom.'

'Really?' She prayed she was projecting coolness and composure, but she could feel her cheeks burning and she doubted it. She couldn't remember ever blushing before she'd met Zak.

'Uh-huh.' His nod and amused, glittering eyes emphasised he, on the other hand, was perfectly in control of himself. 'Unfinished business. I think that describes it, wouldn't you say?'

'I don't think so. As I recall it, we were quite finished.'

'You can be quite daunting when you try,' he observed interestedly. 'Does that come naturally, or do you practise for hours in front of the mirror to get that haughty look?'

His sheer height and breadth was sending delicious little flickers down her spine, but she would rather have died than admit to it. 'Don't be ridiculous,' she said icily.

'But you make me feel ridiculous. You make me want to say something outrageous, shocking, to get past that very secure mask you present to the world.'

Her eyes widened briefly. 'There's no mask.'

'Oh, but there is, and it's made of steel. I would very much like to have met you five years ago, before it was in place. To have seen the woman you used to be then.'

The full import of his words took a moment to register. 'How did you find out?' she said stonily. He knew about Dean.

'Not from your sister or Greg, if that's what you're thinking. I couldn't get a damn thing out of either of them.'

He kept his gaze fixed on her—almost, Blossom caught herself thinking feverishly, as though if he didn't she would bolt for a hole in which to hide herself. Perhaps he wasn't far off the mark at that.

'Fortunately—or perhaps *un*fortunately, in this age of terrorist attacks and other atrocities—the world is a very small place,' Zak said softly. 'Money and determination can buy almost anything. I have both. And I use them when necessary.'

'Bully for you.' Weak, but all she could manage in the circumstances. 'So, now you know.' She eyed him bravely even though she could feel herself shrinking away to nothing. 'Nothing has changed. You knowing makes no difference to me.'

'Perhaps not, but for me it confirms you were only saying what you'd like me to believe all along. It was just the reason for your duplicity I wasn't sure about.'

Blossom reared up as though she had been stung. 'I told you no lies. My career *is* all-important to me. I didn't lie.'

'You were, shall we say, economical with the truth.'

'How dare you?' She couldn't remember when she had been so angry. 'I had no obligation to tell you anything.'

'True.' He moved swiftly, taking her hands in his to prevent her turning away. 'You didn't.'

The muscled strength in his broad shoulders and chest, the uncompromising virility, was both exciting and menacing. 'Let go of me,' she said tightly. She didn't struggle. It would have been useless. 'Let go of me this instant.'

'Only if you promise to talk to me.'

In spite of his words, he let go of her when she demanded

it. Now the burning memory of his hands gripping hers remained with her for several seconds before she could erase the sensations he had caused and bring her mind under control sufficiently to reply. She breathed in and out deeply.

She stared at him with what she hoped was cool aplomb. 'I don't think we've got anything to say to each other.'

'Wrong.' His voice was soft, his face still. 'We've plenty.'

He wasn't going to go away now he was here. It was written all over him. 'You really are the most infuriating man,' she said, more weakly than she would have liked.

'I know.' It was as though she had given him a compliment.

'Would you browbeat a man in the same way?' she snapped, his self-satisfaction catching her on the raw.

'Most definitely.' The blue eyes were laughing now, although his mouth was straight. 'Of course, I've never badgered a man to go out with me—or a woman, come to that,' he added as an afterthought. 'But I don't hold with sexual discrimination on any level, as it happens. I've been accused of many things in my life, and a large percentage of them were probably true, but male chauvinism is not one of them. Now you, on the other hand, are obviously guilty of female chauvinism.'

'What?' She was taken aback and it showed.

'You haven't dated since your divorce. You have a circle of close friends, none of whom are male, and a reputation for freezing men out of the picture if they come on to you. You also have an ability to make a man feel like something that has just slithered out from under a stone. Whatever happened between you and your husband—and my sources informed me he was a less than admirable character'—the steady voice had hardened considerably on the last words—'you now clearly judge all men as wanting. Am I right?' Black eyebrows rose quizzically. 'And don't frown like that, you'll get wrinkles.'

Blossom glared at him. 'You know nothing about me.' This wasn't quite true, she reflected the second the words were out. Unfortunately he seemed to have learnt a great deal about her.

'You mean to say you don't consider the male species less than trustworthy? View them all as wanting?'

You bet your sweet life I do. 'Not at all.' She wished her tone was more scathing. 'I rather suspect your assumption might be due more to the fact I refused to see you again than what you think you might know about me. In my experience, men usually come up with some excuse when their egos are dented.'

'Really?' He smiled lazily, his equanimity unaffected by the slight. 'I wouldn't know, such an unpleasant occurrence has not befallen me, but it sounds somewhat…painful.'

Blossom gave up. 'I'm not prepared to discuss this in the street. Would you like to come in for a coffee?' she asked in a tone which made it clear the invitation was under duress.

'I would like that very much, Blossom,' he said with suspect meekness. 'That is very sweet of you.'

She tossed her head, turning away and walking the step or two to the front door of the house where she inserted her key in the lock. Opening the door, she marched inside without waiting to see if he was following her. The communal staircase was in front of her, but her flat was on the ground floor. Once she had opened the door she stood aside, her voice stiff as she said, 'Please come in.' She watched him as he glanced around.

'This is very pleasant. Restful.' He nodded in approval.

'Thank you.' She didn't add that that was the look she had aimed for with the thick oatmeal carpeting and curtains, and pale-lemon covers in the sitting room. The front door opened straight into the main room, and when she had redecorated the flat she had wanted to create an impression of light and peace in the limited space available. The Victorian terrace had three floors with a flat on each, but the building was narrow, each flat having one main living room, one bedroom, a bathroom and small kitchen. She had painted the walls cream throughout, using overmantel mirrors in the sitting room and bedroom to maximise the space, and keeping the neutral scheme in the kitchen and diminutive bathroom. The somewhat bland theme was offset by the faded grandeur of a few French antiques she, along with Melissa, had inherited from their parents. Zak walked over to her favourite, a fine mirror above the old original fireplace the builder who had converted the house into flats had had the foresight to retain.

'This is beautiful.' He stroked a finger along the gold-painted, intricately carved frame. 'It looks genuine.'

'It is.' She felt ridiculously pleased he liked it so much. 'It belonged to my parents, along with the other pieces.'

'And the garden?' He looked out of the French windows into the small enclosed courtyard beyond, its brick walls painted white and festooned with hanging baskets and trailing plants, providing a festival of colour, in the middle of which her small table and two chairs sat. 'Is it shared?'

'No, it's all mine. The other two flats have balconies. It's tiny, but I love it. I eat out there all the time from spring to autumn.' She stopped abruptly. She was giving too much away. She didn't want him to know anything more about her; he knew far too much as it was. 'I'll make the coffee, or would you prefer a cold drink or a glass of wine?' she asked with studied politeness.

He shrugged. 'Whatever you were going to have.'

She found it hard to believe he was standing here in her home. For the first time in five weeks she felt really alive again. The thought hit at the same time as a little voice in her head said quite clearly, 'He's dangerous. Don't forget it.'

'White wine? There's a bottle chilled in the fridge,' she said with what was admirable coolness in the circumstances.

'Great. Can I open these?' He gestured to the French doors. 'It looks very inviting out there.'

'Be my guest.' She escaped to the tiny kitchen and opened the bottle of wine with trembling fingers. It wasn't a particularly good one; no doubt he was used to the best of the best, but he'd have to like it or lump it.

He seemed to like it. When she returned to the sitting room, Zak was seated at the garden table, one leg crossed over the other and his head back as he soaked up the last of the day's sunshine, and he took a long pull at the wine after she'd handed him his glass. She'd brought out a bowl of peanuts and another of olives which she placed on the table, sitting down herself before she said, 'Zak, I don't mean to be rude, but you must realise by now I'm a lost cause.' She smiled as she spoke, her voice light. She'd determined in the kitchen that was going to be the stance she took—casual, amused, nonchalant.

He didn't reply to this, saying instead, 'What do you do to relax, Blossom—in those rare times you're not working?'

'Relax?' He'd taken her unawares, and she didn't like the sarcasm.

'You do relax occasionally?' he asked silkily.

'Of course I do. Often.' She took a sip of her wine.

'When?' The blue eyes held hers. 'Exactly?'

'What?' She was flustered and it showed.

He sighed, repeating with elaborate—and what Blossom felt was insulting—patience, 'When do you relax?'

'Every evening, weekends...' She took a large gulp of wine. She needed some fortification. He seemed to fill her little garden, dominating the surroundings with unconscious, flagrant masculinity. 'The same times as the majority of the rest of the nation, I suppose. I am quite normal, despite what you think.'

He ignored the jibe. 'And what do you do to relax?'

She'd had enough of this interrogation. Putting down her glass, she leant back in her chair, ticking off on her fingers as she counted, 'Rock climbing, parachuting, canoeing, hang-gliding, judo, potholing.' She narrowed her eyes as though she was thinking. 'Oh, and of course I mustn't forget yoga, pottery, painting, crocheting—'

'No, I'm sorry, but I don't see you as a crocheter,' said Zak, grinning. 'Now, the parachuting and rock climbing...'

In spite of herself she found she couldn't help smiling. 'Well, what do you think I do?' she said, half irritably. 'I read, go to the cinema, to the theatre, the gym—'

'By yourself?' he interrupted, a dry, mordant note to his voice. 'You go to the cinema or the theatre by yourself?'

'There's nothing wrong with being content with your own company,' Blossom returned, warning herself not to rise to the bait. It paid to think before you spoke when dealing with Zak.

He raised a sardonic eyebrow. 'That sounded like something an old lady of ninety might have said.'

Stung, she couldn't help saying, 'I have friends, lots of friends. Of course I go out with them sometimes.'

'That's nice.' He eyed her over the top of his glass.

She could have stamped her foot. Instead she took another

sip of wine before she said, 'I'm perfectly content with my life just as it is. And I like my own company, as it happens.'

'You've already said that,' he reminded her gently.

'Well, I *am*.' He had to be the most irritating man on earth.

'Methinks the lady protests too hard.' And then, before she could come back with the hot retort burning her tongue, he added, 'Melissa's worried about you. You do know that?'

For a moment she couldn't believe he'd said what she thought he had said. Then she drew herself straight in her seat, her voice tinkling ice when she said, 'I don't believe for a moment my sister would discuss me with you. Melissa wouldn't do that.'

'You're right, she didn't. It was something Greg let slip.'

'Greg? Huh.' She glared at him. 'Forgive me for saying so, but Greg might be a whiz at work, in fact I'm sure he is, but delving into the human psyche is so not his style. He forgets anything that isn't remotely connected with electronics within five minutes. Melissa practically has to tie his shoelaces.'

'Which only goes to prove your sister must be pretty concerned if it's registered with him, don't you think?'

The man had an answer for everything. Unfortunately, at this moment in time, she didn't. Blossom stared at him, her brain whirring but without coming up with the put-down she needed— if such a thing existed where Zak Hamilton was concerned.

He leant across the table and touched the side of her face with a gentle finger. 'I'm not trying to be clever,' he murmured, his voice deep and resonant. 'Far from it. But like Melissa I think you need to embrace the real world again. No one can exist in a bubble, Blossom. I tried it myself for a while, so I know what I'm talking about.'

No, don't do this. Don't do tender and warm. Acidic and

confrontational she could handle, but not this other side of him that she had glimpsed once or twice. It was unnerving. Unnerving and dangerously sexy. To combat her weakness her voice was both sharp and brittle when she said, 'Don't tell me—you're just the man to help me "embrace" the world again. Am I right?'

There was a moment of complete silence. His hand had left her face. Then, very slowly, without expression, he said, 'I'm fully aware of how you see me, Blossom. You have me down as an egotist, right? A man full of his own importance who likes to boost his self-assurance by dating one woman after another. Shallow, without moral foundation.'

The world beyond the tiny garden was muted, the low drum of traffic in the streets surrounding them barely impinging on the still, warm air. She didn't know how to answer him. It wasn't in her nature to deliberately hurt another human being, but in all honesty she couldn't deny the charge. She didn't trust him an inch. Whatever he said.

'So it is up to me to prove you wrong,' he said quietly.

Her head had lowered, but now it jerked up as she met his cool gaze. This was not going at all as she'd wanted.

'I've had women, I don't deny it, but not as much as company gossip would declare. Hell, if I'd been as active as my reputation suggests I'd be a mere shell of my former self by now.'

His eyes looked into hers for a few endless moments, and there was no amusement in the sapphire depths. It took a huge effort for her to say evenly, 'This is not funny, Zak.'

'Dead right it isn't.'

He stood up and for a second she thought he was going to leave. Instead he reached out and drew her into his arms, lowering his head and kissing her very thoroughly. She knew she ought to resist. It was crazy not to. So why didn't she—because it was so good to feel like a woman again?

The casual shirt he was wearing was open at the neck and the massive shoulders and muscled chest was accentuated by the thin cotton. The warmth and lemony fragrance from his skin seemed to envelop her, and she had the mad desire to press into him, to slip her arms beneath his shirt and run her fingers over the broad male chest, to bury herself in him.

Whoa there. Whether he sensed her panic or not Blossom wasn't sure, but in the next moment he had put her from him, gazing down at her with inscrutable eyes.

'Don't tell me that didn't hit the right buttons with you, because I know damn well it did,' he said softly. 'We only have to touch each other for bells to go off. Now I don't know about you, but I like that. It's what makes the world go round, after all.'

She shrugged. It was all she could manage.

'I'm thirty-eight years old, Blossom, and I did with playing games a long time ago. I haven't got the patience, for one thing. I like you. I want to see more of you. A lot more.'

She shivered in the warm air.

'We have something going here whether you like it or not. You do accept that?' he said, his piercing eyes never leaving her hot face for one moment. 'Silly question. You can't deny it.'

She hesitated, then said flatly, 'I'm not your type.'

'Really? What *is* my type? Enlighten me.'

She'd caught him on the raw. She recognized it by the way his mouth had thinned and hardened. She shrugged again. 'Women who are happy to enjoy a casual affair with no strings attached for a while and then move on.' Beautiful, expertly groomed, stunning women with the wow factor. Total it-girls.

He nodded noncommittally before saying, 'And your type? What's your type?'

'I don't have a type,' she retorted swiftly, stung he would think so. 'I don't look at people like that.'

'But I do?' He smiled, but it didn't reach the beautiful eyes. 'Your female chauvinism is rearing its ugly little head again. But for your information, Blossom, the only expectation I have of a woman is that she's real. There are too many of the other kind in the crazy world I inhabit. Give me someone who is straightforward, who will say what she really thinks whether she believes I'll like it or not, who doesn't give a damn about my bank balance or whether being seen on my arm notches up her street cred. You fit the bill on all counts, especially in saying what you think,' he added drily.

Did she believe all that? Would any man ignore the original blonde bombshell and opt for the honest little girl-next-door?

'Of course, with you there is the advantage of having a beautiful, sensual, intelligent woman as well as all the facets I've mentioned. Having the cake and eating it.' His eyes held hers, very steady, very calm. 'Even though you don't cook.'

For a moment she could almost believe him. A warmth spread through her and she licked dry lips. If this was a chat-up line, he was very good at it. But then he would be. He'd be good at anything he did. It didn't help much.

'What I'm saying, Blossom, is that I'd like us to get to know each other better. OK?' He took her in his arms again but now he was holding her loosely by the elbows, giving her every opportunity to move away if she so wished. 'We can take it nice and easy. We're both mature adults, there's no rush that I can see. I accept you're wary about getting involved again after your divorce. That's fine. I'm not suggesting we leap into bed here and now. The physical side can happen when you're ready.'

Oh, what should she do? What should she say? She felt in turmoil, so mixed up and confused she could burst into tears any moment. 'I...I want to sit down.' She had to distance herself from the feel of him. She couldn't think with him holding her, even though his touch was as light as thistledown.

Once she was seated Zak sat down too, his gaze intent on her troubled face. 'I think it's only fair to tell you that whatever you say now I have no intention of giving in,' he said calmly. 'Attraction like ours doesn't happen often, and I'm blowed if I'm going to walk away without a fight. I want to get to know you; I want *you* to get to know me. That way we can make an informed decision some time in the future whether to pull the plug or continue to see each other.'

'That sounds very cold-blooded,' Blossom said faintly.

'Cold-blooded? Not a bit of it.' He took a handful of peanuts and ate them before he continued, 'My sources tell me you met and married your husband after just a few weeks, and presumably you lived to regret that?'

She nodded. Regret was far too mild a word.

'What I'm suggesting should therefore be infinitely more...reassuring. A slow courtship. Good old-fashioned word that, courtship, don't you think? Conjures up pictures of girls in straw bonnets and young men standing on the doorstep with a posy in their eager hands. A bygone age.'

His voice was quiet, soothing, and as Blossom stared at him she knew he was deliberately trying to diffuse the situation, create a calm atmosphere. It didn't work, not with him so close. He had said he wouldn't walk away without a fight, and she knew she didn't have the strength to continue to defy him, simply because her head was telling her one thing and her feelings another. Her head said it would be incredibly stupid to let Zak into her life, however limited the contact. Her feelings said she would be mad not to take advantage of what could only be a brief liaison in the overall scheme of things.

Since she had met him thoughts of him had circled her mind constantly whether she'd been awake or asleep. Perhaps it would be better to see him for a time—get him out of her system, so to speak? She agreed the physical attraction between them was fierce, but that was only part of a relationship after all. Maybe when she got to know him she would end up thoroughly disliking him, and then that would make things easy. She knew so little about him, if she thought about it—his views, his slant on politics, religion, life in general. She was sure they wouldn't be compatible, and then she could put him out of her mind and her life for good.

'If we did start seeing each other now and again there would be absolute honesty between us?' She looked at him warily.

'Of course. I told you, I stopped playing games a long time ago. Neither do I apologise for the man I am or make excuses for how I behave.' His gaze was piercingly steady. 'If people don't like it…' He shrugged, settling more comfortably in his seat.

Arrogant. She didn't like arrogance. One on the list. It was a start. 'All right.'

'All right?' Now it was Zak who looked wary. 'All right, meaning…?'

'We could do dinner sometimes, have the odd drink after work, that sort of thing.' Blossom was rather pleased with her casual air. Of course, it would have been nice if the sight of him, relaxed and lazy with his long legs stretched out in front of him and his hand resting idly on his wine glass, didn't make her pulse race and the blood tingle through her veins. But she could work on that. Given time. How much time, she wasn't sure.

'Sounds good to me.' Zak unfurled himself from the chair. 'I'll pick you up at eight. OK?' He smiled lazily down at her.

'What? I didn't mean tonight.' She stared at him, taken aback.

'Why? What are you doing tonight?' he asked with deceptive reasonableness.

Deadpan, Blossom murmured, 'Parachuting. Or is it my rock-climbing class? Darn it, I can't remember in my social whirl.'

'I don't think they hold classes in rock climbing. Must be potholing you're thinking of.'

'That'd be it.' She drained her glass of wine.

'Eight sharp, OK?'

He walked past her and into the flat, ignoring her, 'Hey, hang on a minute, I haven't agreed to…'

Blossom heard the front door bang. 'Go out tonight,' she finished to herself.

Overbearing. Dictatorial. Rude. Three more on the list, and she hadn't even been trying. The list was going to be accomplished in no time at all.

CHAPTER SIX

'So let me get this straight.'

Blossom waited while her sister gave a pregnant pause. She had known this was going to be a difficult phone call, and Melissa wasn't disappointing her. She rarely did.

'You are now going out with the man we both agreed would be majorly crazy, if not one-hundred-per-cent disastrous for you to see. Right so far?' she said tartly.

'I guess,' Blossom said flatly when Melissa let the silence at the other end of the phone grow. 'In a manner of speaking.'

'The man who, far from being your average Mr Nice Guy, is a class-one womaniser? Who has women lined up like skittles?'

'You don't know that.' She didn't know why she was defending Zak. No, actually, she did. 'I don't think his reputation is deserved,' she said carefully. 'Office gossip always embroiders everything, you know that. Not that I'm saying he hasn't known plenty of women, he'd tell you that himself, but I don't think he's any worse than lots of other men.'

'Casanova, Don Juan, men like that?' Melissa put in sweetly.

'Very funny.' She really didn't need this aggravation.

'And the fact that this man who is no worse than lots of other men happens to be drop-dead gorgeous and wealthy and influential and powerful doesn't bother you at all? You feel sure that at heart he's a real one-woman guy?'

Sisters. Why did they always have to put their finger right on the sore bit? 'I don't know,' said Blossom shortly.

'But you're going out with him anyway.'

'Casually.' Blossom paused. 'Strictly on a casual basis.'

There was a snort. It was remarkably eloquent.

'I mean it, Melissa. We're taking it slowly, no strings attached. Just the odd meal now and again. A drink after work.'

'You'll be telling me next the pair of you are just good friends. And please don't. I couldn't stand it.'

'Well, no, I wouldn't go that far, but Zak's fully aware I've got no intention of sleeping with him, if that's what you mean. I've laid it on the line, so there can be no doubt about it.'

'Blossom, Zak Hamilton is the most attractive, sexy man in the universe! How long do you think you're going to hold out? I mean, give me a time span here. A week? A month?'

Blossom breathed out slowly and prayed for patience. 'I thought you didn't like him.'

'That doesn't make me blind.' There was another pause. 'And I've never said I dislike him. I'm just not sure I like him, exactly. That's something completely different.'

'I'm glad we cleared that up.' Blossom shook her head.

'Sis, he's not right for you.' Melissa had changed tack, now her voice was soft and throaty. 'You must see that? I'm only concerned for you. You took such a knock over Dean, I didn't think you were ever going to get over it. And Zak…'

'I know.' She knew all right. Once Zak had deposited her back at the flat after a truly delicious meal at the sort of restaurant she'd only normally got to see from the outside, with her nose pressed up against the windowpane, she hadn't slept all night. One moment she'd been telling herself there was no harm done, she'd only agreed to see him now and again after all, and the next she'd been calling herself every sort of fool.

And—she really wasn't sure if this was a plus or a minus on the list—his goodnight kiss had been a fleeting brush on her lips and nothing else. She had been tied up in knots in the moments before they had reached the flat, wondering how best to make it clear that she intended to stand by all she had said. In the event she hadn't had to say a thing. A brief caress, a murmured, 'I'll ring you tomorrow,' and he had gone. Flipping cheek, when you think about it!

'You say you know, but you don't. That's the whole point.' Not privy to the anticlimatic end to the previous evening, Melissa still had the bit firmly between her teeth. 'Some women might be able to enjoy a brief affair, and say goodbye when the time comes without a moment's regret, but not you. You're not like that. And men are different to us. They can do it without their emotions or heart being involved.'

'Melissa, I hate to point out the obvious, but if anyone knows that, I do,' said Blossom very drily.

'Oh heck! I didn't mean… Dean was just a total swine. It was no reflection on you—'

'It's all right.' She cut Melissa's stammerings short. 'Relax. You haven't mortally wounded me.'

'I'm just concerned about you,' Melissa repeated. 'If it was anyone else but Zak Hamilton you were seeing I'd be over the moon. I just don't want a frying-pan-into-the-fire scenario here.'

'I know that, and I know you've got my best interests at heart. To be truthful this is probably a very bad idea, but at least I know that and I'm on my guard. Honestly, I am. And I'm not expecting it to last two minutes.'

'So why did you agree to go out with him?' Melissa said flatly.

'Excellent question.' With no answer. Just a host of mixed up feelings and emotions she couldn't make sense of. 'Let's just say I was suddenly tired of going out with the girls or on my own.' As the doorbell rang, she said hastily, glad to end the conversation, 'I've got to go, someone at the door. I'll talk to you later.' It was a relief to put down the phone.

After a voice informed her, 'Delivery for Miss White,' on the flat's intercom, Blossom pressed the button and opened the door into the building. When she opened her own front door into the hall, a young lad presented her with an enormous bouquet of deep-red roses and baby's breath, along with a package wrapped in silver paper. She took them a mite gingerly.

Zak. She glanced at the roses with a touch of cynicism, before thanking the boy and closing the door. She didn't have a vase remotely big enough for such an extravagant bouquet. There must be at least fifty stems of roses, besides the baby's breath and fern. It must have cost the earth.

Placing the bouquet on the kitchen worktop, she took the package through to the garden along with a cup of coffee. There had been no card with the flowers, and the reason for this became clear when she opened the parcel to find a book entitled *A Hundred-and-One Reasons For Being Single*, and a message on the flyleaf which read:

Thought this might come in handy this morning, although you're probably up to the hundred mark all by yourself. The flowers are to say there's another side to the coin, that's all. Unless, of course, you're in the habit of sending flowers to yourself? Whatever, treat the flowers with kindness and throw the book in the bin. Zak.

Not 'love, Zak', then. Or 'looking forward to seeing you again'. 'Missing you already' would have been over the top, especially as it was the line Dean had used after their first date when he had sent her flowers. A mixed bouquet, if she remembered correctly, which had already been wilting when she'd received it. She should have known then.

Blossom swallowed. Dean had never had much of a sense of humour. Sending this book wouldn't have occurred to him in a million years. She looked at Zak's writing. It was a black scrawl with a certain flourish to it. It fitted somehow. She groaned inwardly and went to put the flowers in water.

He phoned in the afternoon. She knew it was him even before she picked up the receiver. 'Blossom? It's Zak.'

'Hello,' she said a little breathlessly. 'Thank you for the flowers, they're lovely, and the book provided that one last reason I was looking for. How did you know?'

'It's a gift.'

She could tell he was smiling. She smiled too.

'Doing anything tonight?' he asked lazily.

She had promised herself she would make some excuse not to see him if he asked, practising one or two until she'd been word perfect. 'No, nothing special.'

'Good.' She heard a phone ring in the background and the buzz of voices. He must be phoning from the office even though it was a Saturday. 'Look, there's something of a mini crisis here, and I'll be tied up till gone seven. How about I pick you up once I've finished and we eat together?' he suggested softly. 'Be ready after sevenish or thereabouts.'

A thousand reasons to put a brake on this now. 'OK.'

'See you then.' The receiver went down without further ado.

Blossom sat looking at the phone for a good five minutes,

but she wasn't really seeing it. Eventually she roused herself from the stupor, telling herself she was tired due to the sleepless night, and her whirling thoughts were nothing to do with the deep, silky voice on the other end of the telephone.

She would go and have a shower right now and then take a nap for an hour or two, or else she'd be a wet rag by seven.

The warm water relaxed her aching muscles, and she stood under the flow for some time before drying herself and padding through to the bedroom. Once in bed she was convinced she wouldn't sleep a wink, but the next thing she knew the alarm clock was telling her it was six o'clock. She lay for some minutes in the warm, quiet room. It looked completely different from when Dean had lived here with her. She had redecorated the flat throughout, and the bedroom in particular, even going so far as to buy a new bed, wardrobe and dressing table as well as new bed linen, curtains and carpet. She hadn't been able to bear the thought of sleeping in the bed she had shared with Dean, not after finding out he had used her so completely. For a long, long time she had felt almost dirty, and although she'd known she had done nothing wrong, and that the feeling was ridiculous, it had only been in the last twelve months that the feeling had completely gone.

He had fooled her so utterly, that was the thing. She sat up in bed, brushing her hair out of her eyes and then hugging her knees. Although she had no feeling left for him at all now, beyond disgust and deep loathing, it still unnerved her that she could be taken in so completely. Zak had said she didn't trust the male sex, and that was true up to a point, but she trusted herself—her own intuition and instinct—still less. And she couldn't see that ever changing.

'Don't think about this now.' She spoke out loud into the

pastel-coloured room. 'Enjoy this evening for what it is, a brief interlude.' Because that was all it, and any other dates she might have with Zak, could be. Commitment came at too high a price, and it was one she was not prepared to pay ever again. Nothing and no one was worth becoming vulnerable for, and a relationship couldn't work unless you were prepared to do that.

By the time Zak rang the doorbell at just gone seven, Blossom was ready. She had purposely not dressed up, keeping her clothes pretty but informal. But the sleeveless jersey dress in pale violet was one of her favourites, and the strappy sandals in a deeper shade of violet matched the short-sleeved, buttonless cardigan she'd slung over her arm for later that evening. She had left her hair loose, and it fell in a shining sleek curtain to her shoulders, the wide silver hoops in her ears just visible when she moved her head. It was much too hot to wear make-up, but she'd compromised with a touch of eyeshadow and mascara.

'You look as fresh as a daisy.' Zak smiled at her as she opened the door leading into the street. 'And a hundred times more beautiful.'

'Thank you.' She wondered if he had noticed the little bee brooch pinned to her dress. Melissa had been convinced that what Blossom had assumed was a crystal was actually a diamond, and had actually had the temerity to covertly spirit the brooch away to a jeweller's before Blossom had returned home from her sister's. She had come back utterly unrepentant and full of the fact that she'd been right. It *was* a diamond, and a very nice one, the jeweller had reported. Furthermore, the silver wasn't silver but white gold.

Blossom had been furious with her, but her annoyance was

water off a duck's back to Melissa. She'd merely grinned and turned to Greg, saying, 'He's no skinflint, your esteemed boss. I'll give him that. But then, he *is* loaded after all.'

Perhaps Zak was loaded, Blossom thought now as they walked to the Aston Martin parked outside the house, but it had still been a tremendously generous gift when she'd barely known him.

Once he had settled her in the car, Blossom watched him as he walked round the bonnet to the driver's side. His tie was loose and the first two or three buttons of his shirt undone, and the hard, square jaw bore ample evidence of a strong five-o'clock shadow. His hair wasn't lying as smoothly as the other times she'd seen him; it looked as though he had run his hand through it over and over again.

As he slid into the car, Blossom realised he looked tired. Why this should increase the sensual magnetism at the heart of his attractiveness ten-fold she didn't know, but it did. Perhaps because it suggested a touch of vulnerability in the otherwise ruthless good looks? Whatever, she found her breathing was shallow and her hands damp.

Keeping her voice light and conversational, she said, 'Hard day? You look bushed, if you don't mind me saying so.'

He smiled. 'Let's just say I've had better.' He leant across as he spoke, skimming her bare lips with his mouth before kissing her more deeply. 'Scrub what I said,' he murmured smokily, settling back in his own seat. 'This is a great day.'

Blossom felt a throb of happiness somewhere deep inside. It was probably a line he had used before, she told herself firmly in the next moment, and didn't mean a thing. But still, it was…nice. It didn't help the list thing, though.

'Did you sort out your crisis?' she asked once they had drawn onto the main road and were properly on their way.

He nodded, the hard profile trained on the traffic ahead. 'Unpleasant business,' he said evenly. 'Necessitating immediate action. It came to my attention recently that one of my accountants had been juggling figures. Cooking the books, in other words.'

He glanced at her and Blossom nodded.

'I confronted the individual concerned and he came up with a barrow-load of excuses. Gambling debts, sick mother, heavies on his back for their money, repossession of his house. He tried them all.'

'Was he telling the truth?' she asked curiously.

The sensual mouth thinned. 'That is incidental, as I see it. No one steals from me. Alex was a good enough friend to know that if he'd got problems he could have come and talked with me freely. I knew him at university, damn it. I recruited him myself when I took over the business. Perhaps he thought that gave him an edge, I don't know. Familiarity breeds contempt, maybe?'

Blossom swallowed hard. He was scary when he looked like this. 'What did you do?' she asked, intrigued in spite of herself.

'I threw him to the wolves.'

'The police? You brought the police in?'

He smiled grimly. 'Not the police, no.'

'I don't understand.' She wasn't actually sure if she wanted to, but having started this she didn't seem able to stop.

'I sacked him, having made it clear I'd see that no one else employed him as an accountant. He'll have to do some hard grafting to pay his debts, and he won't like that. He was never someone who liked physical work. He'll be paying off his dues for years to a number of people, me included.'

'What's to stop him just moving away, even leaving the country?' she asked curiously. 'People do that all the time.'

'He won't do that. One or two of the people he's in debt to have very long fingers, and he knows it. No, he'll slog away for little reward with a noose round his neck until he's done, knowing he's wasted his life, lost everything.'

Blossom repressed a shiver. 'The police would have been a kinder option.'

His mouth curved sardonically. 'Kindness wasn't my main priority. And I didn't see why his mother, who happens to be a very nice lady, should suffer the ignominy of having the family name dragged through the mud in the courts.'

'You know his mother?' That made it worse somehow.

'Slightly.' It was succinct.

'Is she really ill like he said?' Blossom persisted.

They had just stopped at traffic lights, and cars surged across the road in front of them. Zak turned to look at her. Patiently, he said, 'Yes, but that has only occurred very recently. He threw it in as a sop.'

'How do you know that?' Ridiculously—because she didn't know this Alex, or his mother either, come to that—she felt tremendous sympathy for them. A young man worried to death about his ailing mother who—foolishly, admittedly, but then no one was perfect—desperately grabs at an improbable straw and starts gambling in an attempt to pay her hospital bills and other expenses. This was awful, just awful.

'She told me,' said Zak as they drew off again.

'She?' Blossom's brow wrinkled.

'Alex's mother.' He changed gear. 'She told me all about it.'

He hadn't worried her with all this when she was ill? Blossom's mental picture of a little old lady sitting wrapped up before a fire, shawl round her shoulders and a bowl of gruel in her lap, went up another notch. Now the woman was racked with sobs. Her son's life had been ruined because of her.

'You went to see his mother and told her her son was a thief?' The list in her head had suddenly got too long to count.

'Not exactly.' It was dismissive.

He hadn't done the job by *telephone*? That made it ten times worse. 'What, then?'

'Does this matter?' The blue eyes raked her face for a second. 'You don't even know the people concerned.'

She didn't know the wife of a man on the news who had been gunned down recently in a random shooting, or the parents of the child on TV last night appealing for a bone-marrow donor, but that hadn't stopped her feeling normal human sympathy and pain for their plight. Something this man apparently was immune to. Stiffly, she said, 'Whether I know them or not isn't the point. You've told me about them now.'

He sighed. 'Are you like this over abandoned puppies too?'

Ignoring that, she said, 'How did you tell his mother?'

'I didn't.' He overtook a family saloon which hooted indignantly.

'But you said…'

'No, Blossom, *you* said,' he returned coolly. 'When his mother came to see me to inform me she had just discovered her son had gambled away the family home, along with syphoning money from the business, we got talking. She was diagnosed with a certain type of leukaemia a few days before.'

'His *mother* told you about Alex?' She stared at him.

'I told you, she's a very nice, honest lady who is mortified by his actions. She had given him the chance to come to me himself, but I think he assumed she was bluffing when she said she'd inform me if he didn't. Another mistake on his part.'

Blossom was lost for words. His mother had turned him in?

'She works with disabled children, after giving up a very highly paid job in the city after Alex's father died some years ago. She felt she wanted to do something positive with the latter part of her life if she couldn't spend it with the man she loved.'

'Oh.' Blossom's voice was small, but not nearly as small as she felt. Thank goodness he didn't know what she'd been thinking.

'Alex persuaded her to make over the house to him some time ago. Avoiding death duties, and so on. She loves her son, and knew nothing about his gambling. She came to see me because she wants him to face up to what he's done and make amends, as much for his sake as anything else. The loss of her home means nothing compared to her son and the mess he's made of his life. I only found out about the leukaemia by chance because she had to leave for an appointment at the hospital treating her. She's not the type of woman to wear her heart on her sleeve.'

Each word on the list had taken on the consistency of a brick as it crashed about her ears. 'Poor lady. Will…will she be all right? With regard to the leukaemia, I mean?'

'I hope so.' Again it was dismissive.

'But where will she live if the home is going to have to be sold to pay some of his debts?'

'I own some property.'

'You do?' His voice had been reluctant, he clearly didn't like revealing his philanthropy. 'Will she be able to afford the rent?' The poor woman was practically destitute, after all.

He shifted irritably in his seat. 'She'll be living there rent-free for the forseeable future.'

Wow. She was so, *so* thankful he hadn't been able to read her mind earlier. She sat quiet for a moment or two and then couldn't resist asking, 'What about Alex? Where will he live?'

'Alex can go to hell.'

Right. Well, she couldn't blame him. Perhaps it was time to change the subject, though, all things considered.

They talked of inconsequentials as the car nosed through the heavy traffic. It was ten minutes before Blossom asked tentatively, 'Where are we going, exactly?' She was wondering if she should have dressed up a bit more.

'Exactly?' His mouth quirked. 'Just a little place I know in Harrow. You'll like it. It's very informal.'

'Harrow? What's it called?' Not that she knew Harrow at all.

'Hamilton's place.'

'Hamilton's Place? That's a coincidence, isn't it, with your name being…?' Her voice trailed to a stop. 'It's your home,' she accused flatly. 'We're going to your home, aren't we?'

'Do you mind?' He glanced at her for a moment. 'I've been in this shirt all day, and would love a shower and a change of clothes before we eat.'

Put like that she could hardly refuse. 'No, that's fine.' She paused. 'Where are we going to eat?'

'I thought we could let my housekeeper look after us,' he said lazily. 'It's been a long day, and I didn't feel like making the effort to go out when Geraldine's cooking is so good. It means I can have a couple of glasses of wine with my meal and get Will to drive the car later.'

'Will being?' Suddenly the evening had changed.

'Geraldine's husband. He does the gardening and odd jobs, and acts as chauffeur when I need him to. They've been with me for years, since I bought the house. They're a great couple.'

'They live in?' She wasn't aware of the relief threading her voice. Of course, he picked up on it straightaway.

'Yes, they live in,' he said very drily. 'So you are quite safe, my lamb, even if you are about to walk into the big bad wolf's lair.'

Blossom's throat tightened. Had she been that obvious? 'I don't know what you mean,' she said quickly.

'Of course you don't,' he said soothingly.

Blossom wanted to kick him. Instead she contented herself with looking regally out of the window for the rest of the journey until Zak swung the car off the road, through some open wrought-iron gates and into a long drive.

Blossom became aware her mouth had fallen open, and shut it with a little snap. The drive was perhaps fifty yards long, bordered by bowling-green-smooth lawns and flower-beds that blazed with colour in the warm evening, but it was the truly beautiful building at the end of it that took her breath away. The house was huge, built of mellow, honey-coloured stone and topped with a thatched roof, below which leaded-glass windows glittered and twinkled in the late sunshine. It was a dream of a house, she thought wondrously, a romantic fairy-tale of a place, and totally not the sort of home she'd imagined the big, hard, very male man at the side of her would have chosen.

'Like it?' Zak asked softly as they drew closer.

'It's exquisite.' There was no other word for it. 'When did you buy it?'

'Twelve months after I took over the business. It was a risk at the time. I wasn't sure how things were going to go, because my father had run the business down before he died, and although I'd got a few things in the pipeline it wasn't the sensible time to take out a massive mortgage on a property which needed a hell of a lot of work doing to it. But I saw it and I wanted it.' He turned, his eyes stroking over her face. 'And when I want something I'll do anything to get it.'

Two huge beech-trees stood either side of the house like sentinels on duty, their shade reaching down to the sun-splotched, kidney-shaped parking area directly in front of the broad stone steps leading to the wide front door.

As Zak cut the engine, he continued, 'Fortunately the business took off big time, and within a year or two all the work was finished and I could relax and enjoy the place. It's my bolthole, my bit of sanity in what is often a crazy world. This is where I'm me, you know?'

'It's a wonderful environment to be you in,' she said lightly, wondering how many other women he'd brought to his home. Dozens, no doubt. Hundreds.

'I know it.' He opened his door and slid out of the car, walking round to her side and helping her out. 'Come on, come and meet Geraldine and have a look round. There's a swimming pool at the back, if you fancy a dip.'

Taken aback, she said, 'I didn't bring a swimming costume.'

'Damn.' He grinned. 'Skinny dipping it'll have to be, then. I won't look if you won't. Fair?'

'I don't think so.' He'd taken her hand as he led her up the wide circular steps, and her heart was pounding like a sledge-hammer. 'Anyway, I'm too hungry to swim.'

'Next time, then.'

The sledgehammer intensified. He wanted there to be a next time. She warned herself that didn't mean a thing.

When he opened the door Blossom had prepared herself for grandeur, but the wooden-floored hall wasn't just grand, it was heart-stirring. Or at least it stirred her heart, she thought whimsically. Light, plain walls with the odd painting dotted here and there, huge bowls of flowers on small tables close to the two sofas the hall held and—something which really provided the magic touch—a magnificent grandfather clock gently dozing in one corner, casting a benevolent eye over the whole.

Sunlight spilled into the hall from two large windows either side of the front door, and the whole feeling the house gave was one of warmth and peace and honey-coloured space.

A door opened at the far end of the passageway on the right-hand side of the wide, curving staircase, a small white-haired woman bustling out. 'I thought I heard the car.' The little rosy-cheeked face was smiling. 'And you must be Miss White. How do you do?' she said, holding out her hand.

'Call me Blossom, please.' As Blossom shook hands with the housekeeper she was aware of a pair of bright brown eyes looking at her very intently. 'It's nice to meet you.'

'You too, dear.' Geraldine smiled, before turning to Zak and saying, 'I've run you a bath, so why don't you get off upstairs and let me show Blossom round? All this with that so-called friend of yours has done you in, hasn't it? You look ready to drop. Go and soak for a few minutes.'

It was for all the world as though she was Zak's mother, or perhaps grandmother would be a better description, because the little woman looked to be in her late seventies at least. Blossom watched with hidden amazement as Zak reached out and touched the housekeeper's lined cheeks, his voice soft as he said, 'Bossy as always. Perhaps Blossom would rather I show her the house. Have you thought of that?'

'And perhaps she'd rather eat before midnight.'

'I'd love Geraldine to show me round,' Blossom intervened. 'You go and freshen up and I'll see you in a few minutes.' The truth was she needed a short time to collect her thoughts without his unsettling presence dominating her mind. She was seeing another side to him here, an even more disturbing side than she had seen thus far. He couldn't have been more gentle or tender with the housekeeper if she *had* been his grandmother. That, combined with the knowledge Zak had provided a home for the mother of this friend who had been stealing from him, just didn't fit the mental picture she'd had of the powerful boss of Hamilton Electronics.

It was annoying, terribly annoying, but Zak wouldn't stay in the box she had designated for him, and the more she learned about him the more he got under her skin.

His home was vast—eight bedrooms all with *en suites*, along with three reception rooms, a huge kitchen, utility room, breakfast room and dining room, and an extension holding the indoor swimming pool at the side of which, reached by a separate passageway, was the housekeeper's apartment. Geraldine showed Blossom all of it, apart from the master-bedroom suite.

After the tour Blossom found herself deposited in the modern cream-and-gold drawing room which was all soft, plumpy sofas, gold silk draperies and cushions, and dominated by a magnificent cast-stone fireplace and antique gilt mirror. The room was almost exactly as she would have furnished it, given a free hand, and this in itself was disturbing.

She sat waiting for Zak in the sun-dappled surroundings with a glass of wine in her hand, wondering all the time what on earth she was doing here. She stared out of the huge bay windows, her gaze focusing on a weeping willow, and then the general grounds surrounding the house which Geraldine had informed her amounted to half an acre, all enclosed by tall evergreens.

Putting down the glass, she walked across to the windows and flung one open, breathing in the air which was subtly scented with the perfume of pine and flowers. It was so clean and fresh, the sun warm on her face. It was hard to believe she was still in greater London because it was so quiet, only the happy chirping of the birds in the trees surrounding the garden breaking the peace, and they merely accentuated the overall tranquility. Suddenly, and without warning, Blossom felt immensely sad, bereft even, as though she had lost something precious with no hope of ever finding it.

Horrified to find tears pricking at the backs of her eyes, she leant against the windowsill, taking great, soothing breaths of the fragrant air. This was crazy, insane. She was in beautiful surroundings, sipping excellent wine and about to enjoy a good meal. What was there to feel wretched about?

'Peaceful, isn't it?'

Zak's voice just behind her caused her to swing round in alarm. How long he had been there watching her she had no idea. 'It's lovely,' she said inadequately, forcing a smile.

He didn't move away. Instead he turned her round so her back was against his front, putting his arms loosely round her as he said, 'You see that big pine tree on the right? There's a family of wood pigeons nesting there. The nest is such a rickety affair it's a wonder it can hold the two fat babies inside. They were ugly little devils when they were first born, all beak and skin, but they've come on since then.'

Blossom swallowed hard. He smelt divine, and the brief glimpse she'd had of him in black jeans and black open-necked shirt, the sleeves rolled up revealing hard, sinewy arms, had told her he looked as sexy as temptation itself.

'At night we have a barn owl that does the rounds; you'll perhaps hear him later. He tends to sit on the roof warning off intruders,' Zak continued softly. 'He's a big fellow, and aggressive with it—his territory, and all that.'

Blossom swallowed again. Wrapped round with his male warmth as she was, it was difficult to breathe normally, the ache in her throat and tightness in her chest constricting. 'It's like you're in the country here,' she managed to say at last. 'The city with all its noise seems light-years away.'

'That's true,' Zak murmured, his chin nuzzling the silk of her hair as he spoke. 'It's a beautiful spot; I'm a very lucky man. A very lucky man,' he repeated huskily, his arms tightening their hold on her softness.

She knew he was aroused by her closeness; his body bore ample evidence of that as he held her against his hard flesh, and he was breathing fast as he shifted her to face him again. He put his mouth to hers, one hand in the small of her back to steady her, and the other lightly cupping her breast through the thin material of her dress. She shivered, her mouth opening involuntarily, and immediately the kiss deepened, his tongue taking the undefended territory and creating raw, hot desire that ripped through her nerve endings with bewildering heat. His fingers were slowly moving over her taut nipple, gently, erotically, in the same way his mouth was moving over hers, his thighs hard as he fitted her into him.

She had never felt this way with Dean. The thought was there in the tiny part of her mind still functioning rationally. She had enjoyed their love-making—looked forward to it, even—but it hadn't produced this raging, primitive passion that was outside her imagination, her mind, herself, everything, a live entity that had to be fed or she would die.

'Delicious…' His throaty growl stroked her as he put her from him, and it was only then Blossom became aware of the knock at the drawing-room door. 'OK?' he asked softly, and as she nodded dazedly, he left her, walking across the room and opening the door himself.

As she turned to face the window again, struggling for composure, she heard Zak talking to Geraldine, but it was beyond her to acknowledge the conversation. It was a moment or two before the housekeeper left, and by then she was more in control, although she knew her cheeks were still flushed and burning. She felt nervous and exhilarated and not a bit like herself.

'Dinner in five minutes.'

She forced herself to face Zak as he spoke. 'Great.' She aimed for matter-of-factness. 'I'd love to see the garden, if that's all right?' she added, walking across and picking up her wine glass. No more cosy togetherness if she could help it.

'Sure.' He poured himself some wine from the bottle Geraldine had placed next to some nibbles on the coffee table. 'We'll take our wine with us. It's nice out there in the fresh air.'

Blossom breathed a little easier once they were outside. The summer twilight had turned the garden into pools of shadow and sunlight, streaks of pink beginning to trickle into the bright blue sky. The white and sugary pink of the magnolia blossoms, the rich scent from the flowerbeds, and deep green of the lawn soothed her shattered senses as they slowly walked round the grounds. 'This was an overgrown jungle when I bought the house,' Zak said quietly. 'But Will's a keen gardener, and he discovered a beautifully laid out garden beneath the weeds and elephant-high grass. A good tree surgeon and lots of TLC from Will, and it was restored to its former splendour.'

As though on cue a tall, lean man with snow-white hair and a deeply tanned face entered the garden from a narrow side gate set between the house and garage block, two large Dobermanns on leads at his side. Blossom eyed the dogs with alarm.

'Here's Will now.' Zak raised a hand in greeting. 'He always takes the dogs for a long walk about this time. I'll introduce you. You don't mind dogs, do you?' he added as Will bent down and let them loose. 'These two are softies at heart.'

Dogs, no. Dogs masquerading as small ponies with great, slavering jaws, question mark. And softies—with those teeth?

Blossom had to admit the dogs were very well behaved, though. She heard Will give a command, and instead of them galloping towards her as she had feared they walked with sedate docility at the side of the gardener, rolling over to have their tummies rubbed as soon as they reached Zak. 'Blossom, meet Will. Will, Blossom. And the two clowns at my feet are Thor and Titus. They're supposed to be guard dogs, but no one has let them into the secret. Will, least of all.'

Will smiled at Blossom. 'Pleased to meet you,' he said equably. 'And don't take any notice of him. If anyone was foolish enough to enter the house without invitation, they wouldn't do it a second time. They're just not aggressive, that's all.'

Blossom smiled back. Will obviously had the same easy-going relationship with Zak as his wife did. 'Have you trained them yourself?' she asked, her gaze returning to the two dogs, who were now politely sniffing the hand she'd extended.

Will nodded, ignoring the snort Zak had given at the mention of training. 'From pups. And forget all the tales you might have heard about dangerous dogs. These two love people, and they just plain love playing with kids. Good as gold with them.'

'That's because they think they *are* kids.' Zak shook his head. 'There are two perfectly good kennels out here which have never been used. Instead two baskets mysteriously appeared in the house complete with feather cushions.'

Blossom had noticed the ecstatic greeting the big dogs had given Zak, and the way he had crouched down to fuss over them before straightening. She suspected Will wasn't the only one who spoilt the duo.

The two men continued to chaff each other as the three of them walked to the house, where Geraldine met them. 'Come and eat, it's all ready,' she said, Will disappearing in the direction of the kitchen with Thor and Titus at his heels.

The dining room's leather armchairs were very comfortable, and the first course of carrot, ginger and honey soup absolutely delicious, but Blossom found she hardly tasted it, she was in such a state. She had been rash to agree to eat at his home. Rash to be tempted by the thought of a further glimpse into his life. Because that was what *had* tempted her, sure enough. She should have known by now it would only further confuse her.

After Geraldine had bustled out with their empty soup dishes, she finished her glass of wine as her thoughts churned on. If she had stuck to her guns in the first place, brushed him off no matter how persistent he'd become, she wouldn't be in this mess. And she should never have allowed him to kiss her. More than that, she should never have kissed him back. But she had. Along with allowing more intimacy…

'The soup wasn't to your liking?'

She raised startled eyes to find the blue gaze studying her with piercing thoroughness, a frown bringing the dark brows together. 'No, it was delicious.' She nodded her head for extra emphasis. 'Absolutely delicious.'

'But you don't like the wine?' he persisted silkily.

'Of course I do.' She nodded again. 'It's excellent.'

'Then what is it?'

'What's what?' she asked with ungrammatical abruptness.

'The reason for looking as though you've lost a pound and found a penny.' He leant back in his chair, eyes narrowed.

'I wasn't.' She probably had been.

'Then everything is fine?'

She didn't answer immediately, and his frown deepened. Then she said slowly, 'I shouldn't have come here, Zak. We shouldn't be seeing each other. It's going to get too... complicated. You know it is. You must be able to sense it too?'

To her surprise the frown smoothed to a quizzical ruffle. 'Is that all?' The frown disappeared altogether. 'That's it?'

'All?' Here she was turning inside out, and he said was it all. Men were unfeeling brutes, the whole lot of them. 'It's enough.'

'It's only going to get as complicated as we want it to,' he said reasonably. 'As *you* want it to. You can cool it any time.'

Right now that was no help. Not the way she was feeling.

'Have some more wine.' He leant over and refilled her glass, and she wondered if his children would inherit his sexy mouth. And the eyelashes. They were really to-kill-for.

Warning herself to go easy on the wine, Blossom said, 'Do you always bring your girlfriends home for dinner?' She hadn't meant to say that, she thought in horror the next moment. Where had that popped up from? He'd think she was jealous or something.

Zak didn't seem at all perturbed. A small smile lifting the corners of that oh-so-sexy mouth, he said, 'No.'

'Oh.' She stared at him. Was he going to elaborate? A number would be nice—nine out of ten? Five? Two?

By the time Geraldine returned with their main course, the silence had become painful, at least to Blossom. Not so Zak, it would appear. He appeared perfectly relaxed, utterly chilled.

'Great.' He stared at his plate happily. 'No one does Cashel Blue steak like Geraldine. You're in for a treat.'

If all he could think about was his stomach... Blossom glared at him. He didn't seem to notice. And the food did smell out of this world. She looked at her steak, and the roasted new-potatoes and steamed French beans reposing beside it. Picking up her knife and fork, she began to eat.

Two glasses of wine and a double helping of apple cookies-and-cream crumble later, Blossom was finally relaxed. Zak had suggested to Geraldine that she and Will join them for coffee in the drawing room, when the housekeeper had cleared their dessert bowls, and now the four of them were sitting round a plate of Geraldine's buttery shortcake, sipping the sort of coffee Melissa would definitely have approved of.

In fact, her sister would have approved of Geraldine altogether. The housekeeper made all her own bread and biscuits, was a devotee of everything organic, and didn't know the meaning of the world instant. Moreover, she was *interesting*. She and Will. The pair of them had travelled all over the world while waiting for the baby that had never happened, spending a year in this country and eighteen months in that, never putting down roots and just earning enough to pay their way. A nomadic existence right up to their sixties.

'But we were happy, weren't we, love?' Will said quietly,

looking at his wife in a way that brought a lump to Blossom's throat. 'Still are. We've had a charmed life.'

'That's true.' Geraldine smiled back at her husband. 'We've never had a penny to our name, and if we hadn't met Zak when we did I doubt we'd be as comfortable as we are now, but we'd have got by. As long as we'd got each other.'

Lucky, lucky things. Blossom stared at them, envying the couple with all her heart. She didn't usually let herself dwell on the solitary future she had been forced into, but tonight it seemed to stretch before her like a great black hole.

Then Zak entered the conversation, saying something wicked which made them all laugh, and the moment passed by. Nevertheless, it left an ache in her heart region she couldn't shift. An uncomfortable pain that coloured the rest of the evening.

It was past one o'clock in the morning when Will finally made noises about driving Blossom home. Looking at her watch, she was mortified to think she had left it so late for the elderly man; time had slipped by without her being aware of it. 'It's so late, Will. I'm so sorry. Please let me call a taxi. By the time you've driven me home and then come back here, it'll be time for breakfast.'

'A slight exaggeration.' Will smiled. 'And I wouldn't hear of it. It won't take two tics.'

It would take a great deal more than two. 'Please, I'd feel much better.' She appealed to Zak when Will shook his head. 'I don't want to drag Will out at this time of night.'

'This time of the *morning*,' said Zak. 'It's tomorrow already.'

Not helpful. And he couldn't drive, having had three glasses of wine with the meal and then a brandy with his coffee. Not that it had affected him in the slightest, from what she could determine. The intimidatingly intelligent mind hadn't seemed anything but razor-sharp as always.

Blossom felt she had been proved right on that score when Zak said quietly and without much expression. 'Why don't you stay the night? There's any one of a number of bedrooms to choose from, and Geraldine does a mean Sunday lunch.'

Blossom looked at him. She might be wrong—possibly, *maybe*—but she'd bet everything she owned that he had purposely let the evening get so late with a view to putting this particular suggestion. She had played right into his hands. If she hadn't said anything, ten to one he would have made some comment about it being late for Will himself.

'I couldn't possibly,' she said firmly. 'But I insist on calling a taxi. There are plenty available at the weekends.'

'I wouldn't hear of it.' Will entered the conversation again. Lovely though he was, Blossom could have strangled him. 'I'll drive.'

For goodness' sake! Blossom looked at Geraldine, but she got no help from that quarter. Instead the small woman smiled brightly. 'The beds are aired in all the rooms.'

Was this a conspiracy? Blossom scrutinised the older couple and then felt ashamed of herself. No, of course it wasn't, but she was sure Zak had manoeuvred the lot of them. 'I haven't any night things,' she said quickly. 'I didn't bring anything.'

'There are spare toothbrushes and toiletries in all the guest bedrooms, along with bathrobes and so on.'

If Geraldine thought she was being helpful, she wasn't. 'That's very kind, but I really would prefer to go home.'

'That's no problem.' Will stood to his feet. Zak eyed her in a 'how could you do such a thing?' way, but said nothing.

Blossom admitted defeat. 'Well, if it's really no trouble to stay…' She cast her host a baleful look.

'Bless you, of course it isn't,' said Geraldine cheerfully. 'And Zak normally has breakfast in bed with the Sunday papers. Is that all right?'

'What?' For a moment Blossom's mind went into hyperdrive.

'If I bring you a tray about nine?' Geraldine didn't seem to notice her flaming cheeks, for which Blossom was inutterably thankful. 'And you'd probably be more comfortable in the blue room; it's got a wonderful view of the garden from the balcony.'

'Yes, yes, that'd be lovely, but you don't need to wait on me, I can easily come downstairs to the kitchen.' Blossom could hear herself babbling, and could see Zak was trying not to smile out of the corner of her eye. He knew exactly how she was feeling, and he was relishing every minute of it. The rat.

'No, no. I'll bring you a tray. It's what we do at weekends.'

She had obviously said the wrong thing; Geraldine looked askance. Blossom glanced at Zak who smiled back cheerfully. She wasn't going to win tonight. 'Well, thank you,' she said to Geraldine. 'That would be lovely, if it's no trouble.'

'No trouble at all. Do you want me to show you the room now?' Geraldine said helpfully.

'Don't worry, Geraldine,' Zak intervened, his voice silky-smooth. 'You and Will get off to bed. I'll settle Blossom in.'

Blossom stood up as the other two left the room. There was no way she was staying down here with him alone. It wasn't that she didn't trust him—although she didn't, and if tonight was anything to go by she had good reason to think that way—but that she didn't trust herself. That little interlude before they had gone out into the garden had told her she was a pushover where Zak Hamilton was concerned, and being a pushover once in her life had been more than enough.

Zak surveyed her through glittering eyes. 'Want a nightcap?' He gestured at the decanter of brandy. 'Or a port, perhaps?'

'No thank you.' She kept her gaze steady. He knew *she* knew he had manipulated her into staying the night, but she was darned if she was going to give him the satisfaction of mentioning it. He'd deny it anyway. Or probably not, she amended in the next breath, which would be worse, forcing her to go down a path she had no intention of treading. 'I'm tired; I'm ready for bed.'

'Me too.'

He stood up, and every muscle and sinew in her body registered the movement. To combat her appalling weakness, Blossom said briskly, and with more than a touch of desperation, 'Geraldine and Will are very nice, aren't they?'

'Very nice,' he agreed gently.

'It must be lovely to know you've given such nice people a home and security in their latter years.'

'Lovely.' He nodded, his blue eyes caressing her mouth.

'Zak—'

'Yes?' He'd moved closer.

She shivered. 'I don't want…'

'What don't you want?' The words were a breath on her face. 'Tell me what you don't want, my skittish beauty. Or perhaps…tell me what you *do* want.'

She clung to the last remnant of reason. 'I want to go to bed.'

'So do I, sweetheart. So do I.'

CHAPTER SEVEN

When Blossom awoke the next morning to a knock on the bedroom door she didn't know where she was for a moment. Then it all came flooding back. This was Zak's house. She was in his bed—well, one of them—and owing to the fact that she hadn't worn a slip under her dress the day before she was stark naked under the summer duvet. *And*—she wriggled slightly—he had been a perfect gentleman when he had shown her to her room the night before. A brief stroking of her sealed lips and that had been all. Which was good. *Very* good, she reiterated, frowning. It meant she hadn't needed to send him packing.

Mind you… She fitted the duvet more closely round her. It would have been…polite for him to have shown a bit more enthusiasm. He was a master at blowing hot and cold.

The knock came again, and with the duvet wrapped round her Blossom sat up against the thick pillows ready for when Geraldine carried the tray in. 'Come in,' she called, feeling a bit awkward at the elderly woman waiting on her like this.

Except it wasn't Geraldine outside after all.

'Hi.' Zak was wearing a black silk robe and matching pyjama bottoms, and he had obviously taken a shower because his black hair was still quite damp. He had had a shave too. As he came closer that seemed more intimate than anything, somehow.

He was carrying the breakfast tray, a folded paper placed to one side of the food, and as he neared the bed he said, 'Sleep well? Bed comfy?'

'Yes, thank you.' Somehow she got the words out of her dry mouth. He had a magnificent body and the black silk emphasised it.

'Good.' He smiled, then settled the tray on her lap. She held on hard to the duvet. 'It's nice to see you first thing in the morning,' he said softly, kissing her.

She wished she'd had time to brush her teeth, comb her hair and check she'd got all her mascara off the night before. A panda-eyed scarecrow wasn't much of a turn-on.

'There's a full English breakfast under there.' He pointed to the covered plate next to the rack of toast and orange juice. 'Geraldine's a great believer in a hearty breakfast.'

'So I see.' She had never felt so vulnerable in all her life. At least he had *some* clothes on. Not much, admittedly.

'Once you've eaten and showered, I thought we might visit an antique fair that's on this morning not far from here. Interested?' He didn't seem to notice her agitation.

'Great.' She nodded carefully. Sudden movement wasn't an option, what with the tray and her need to keep the duvet firmly in place. Her fingers tightened on the material.

He looked at her for one more moment, a long look. Then he walked to the door, murmuring over his shoulder, 'Your ex was the biggest fool out, and it's galling to admit I've reason to be grateful to him.'

'What?' She didn't follow.

He turned after he had opened the door, standing with his

hand on the handle as he said, 'But for his stupidity you wouldn't be here right now, would you?' And then he closed the door quietly behind him, leaving her staring into space.

Once Blossom had showered and dressed she felt more in control. She had eaten every morsel of Geraldine's delicious breakfast, and now welcomed the fact they were going to go out; she needed to walk off a few calories if she was going to do justice to lunch. The spare tyre was threatening again.

Zak was waiting for her in the hall when she came downstairs with the breakfast tray.

'You needn't have brought that; Geraldine would have collected it,' he said, taking the tray from her when she reached the bottom of the stairs. 'You're my guest.'

'Guest or not, I don't expect Geraldine to fetch and carry for me. My legs are younger than hers.'

'They're more shapely too.' He grinned at her, his eyes accentuated by the sky-blue shirt he was wearing. The smile faded as he said softly, 'But thanks for the thought. She's no spring chicken, although she'd take me apart if she heard me say that. I'm always telling her to slow down a bit.'

Once Zak had taken the tray through to the kitchen and they had exited the house into the bright summer sunshine, Blossom said quietly, 'What will you do, Zak, when Geraldine and Will are too old to work for you any longer?'

He glanced at her as he opened the passenger door, but it wasn't until he was seated in the car that he said, 'The apartment is their home, I built it for them. Geraldine chose all the furnishings and fittings herself, and the garden is Will's pride and joy. I see them finishing their days here. They're not employees, Blossom, they're…' He paused.

'Family?' she said very quietly. It was plain how he felt.

'I guess.' He shrugged. 'Yes, they're family to me.'

She glanced at him, remembering his experience of family life hadn't exactly been a good one. He looked very big and commanding as he started the car, in control of himself and the world in general. So why did she suddenly want to put her arms round him, not in a romantic sense, but in a desire to comfort the little boy he had once been? The boy who had been rejected by his nearest and dearest and who had been forced to stand on his own two feet at far too young an age.

She turned her head to the window, willing the compassion to subside. It was too dangerous an emotion to indulge in where Zak was concerned. *He* was too dangerous.

The antique fair was fun, or rather wandering round the stalls and tables hand in hand with Zak was fun. And disturbing. For the first time in a long while, she felt like anyone else, the sign on her forehead which read 'unlovable' missing for once. In fact she felt young and attractive, and she must have given off some sort of aura which projected this because she noticed more than one male give her a second glance.

Zak dived on a beautiful little Meissen model of two recumbent Dobermanns on the very last stall they visited, the price of which made Blossom blink. The model was naturalistically coloured, and had been lovingly restored in parts, the two dogs the very image of Thor and Titus. After a few minutes of haggling with the somewhat scary-looking matron manning the stall, Zak got a couple of hundred pounds knocked off the asking price and bought the model. He looked very pleased with himself.

'For Geraldine and Will,' he explained as they strolled away. 'It's their golden wedding anniversary at the end of the month, and I've been looking for something special for weeks. Geraldine started collecting Meissen a few years ago, but she hasn't anything like this. They'll love it; those dogs are their babies.'

She smiled. His generosity to the old couple touched her, but made her feel a little uneasy too. It was easier to keep him at arm's length in her emotions when he was the cold-hearted, ruthless, 'love 'em and leave 'em' boss of Hamilton Electronics as portrayed by Melissa. The fact that Melissa's opinion was based largely on hearsay she chose to put to the back of her mind.

Once in the car, Zak didn't start the engine straight away. Instead he leaned forward, not touching her with any part of himself, yet enveloping her with his male warmth. 'What happened with your ex?' he asked very softly. 'Don't tell me if it's still too painful to talk about, but I'd like to understand.'

She stared at him, utterly taken aback, then rallied enough to say flatly, 'I thought you knew all about it from the person you hired to find me.'

'No, just bare facts, that's all. You married, he left seven months later and there was another woman involved. He was a model, and according to my source his star began to ascend when he met you. I take it that wasn't coincidence?'

Blossom looked down at her hands in her lap. 'No, it wasn't,' she said tonelessly. 'I was a means to an end to Dean, that's all. Our marriage was a sham from the start. Of course, I didn't know that until he walked out on me after clearing my bank account for him and the woman he'd been living with when he met me. She was another secret he kept well hidden.'

She raised her eyes, looking him straight in the face. 'The funny thing is, I thought we were perfectly happy. I was convinced I had a great marriage. Looking back, I can see all sorts of cracks, but at the time…' She shook her head. 'Gullible doesn't even begin to describe it, does it?'

'No.' He looked at her searchingly. 'What describes it is a trusting, warm good person being taken in by a lying, shallow cheat. You weren't gullible, Blossom. Not in the way you mean. You believed in someone because they projected an image they wanted you to see. And if someone is cunning and immoral enough, if they are without basic human dignity and ethics, they will always be able to fool the sweet and honourable who want to believe the best in folk. But only for a time. Dean will reap what he's sown one day. I've seen it time and time again, both in business and life.'

Blossom shrugged. 'I don't think I believe that—with regard to Dean, I mean. He could charm the birds out of the trees without even trying. The original golden boy. You know?'

'And when the charm gets a trifle worn? When the good looks fade, and the jowls sag, and the six-pack turns to fat? There are no real-life Peter Pans, Blossom. Just embarrassingly and increasingly desperate no-hopers chasing an illusion.'

'He's got years and years before that will happen, if it ever does.' She shook her head. Dean would always come up trumps.

'Oh it will, you can count on it. And in the meantime what does he have—*really* have? He's thrown away the one thing in his life which would have taken him out of the norm and made him a king. One day he'll realise it, and it might be sooner than you think. My informant told me he's not been doing so well the last year or two. Did you know that?'

She shook her head. His words had fallen like balm on the scars on her self-esteem and confidence, but strangely they had made her heart ache. The feeling was similar to the one she'd experienced the night before, when she had stood at the window and looked out into the fragrant twilight, but this time she understood it a little better. The pain was for what might have been. If she had met Zak before Dean, if she had never got married and been betrayed so completely, if she was still the person she had been then… But she wasn't. She had changed, she knew she had. Irrevocably. She would never know a moment's peace with a man like Zak, and having clawed her peace of mind back inch by agonising inch she wasn't about to throw it away. It was more precious to her than anything. Or anyone.

'What would you do if he contacted you again?' Zak asked quietly, his eyes never leaving her face. 'Would you meet him?'

She shrugged again. 'I don't know,' she said honestly. 'I do know I have no feeling left for him beyond disgust. I hated him at one point, and I clung on to that for a long time. It was a weird sort of comfort—it told me I was still able to feel. You know?'

He nodded. He said nothing, but continued to watch her face.

Blossom didn't know if he understood or not; she barely did herself. 'But then I realised I was hurting no one but myself. I was becoming something I disliked. So I went for therapy, as Melissa had been asking me to do since it happened. I poured out my soul to my therapist, wrote letters to Dean which I read out to her and then we burnt them. We even went to a quiet spot on the Thames one day, and I threw stones into the water which represented all my feelings of rage and hatred and hurt.' She smiled a small smile. It all seemed so long ago now, and yet it had only been a few months since she'd stopped seeing her therapist. All the bitterness finally had gone.

'Did it work?' Zak asked gently.

'Amazingly, yes.' There was a tenderness in his eyes, which was increasing the ache, and she had to look away. She focused her gaze on a huge oak tree some distance away, its leaves lit by the sunshine. It was a magnificent tree, probably over a hundred years old, Blossom thought. It had been standing in the same place all the time, and below its spreading branches the lives of men and women had gone on. Births, marriages, deaths. Heartache, happiness. All fleeting.

'I'm glad.' Zak bent over and kissed her full on the lips. He didn't prolong the embrace—they were in a car park outside the antique market, after all—but when he settled back in his own seat their eyes met. The gentleness had gone from his gaze; now there was a deep glow which turned the blue to dark violet, and she couldn't look away. It held her, shaking her to the very core as something deep within herself leapt to meet the banked desire. A warmth trickled through her blood, frightening and exciting at the same time. The atmosphere within the car had become electric, quivering with something unnameable, something elemental, something terrifying.

Blossom wrenched her eyes from his, panic uppermost. Whatever he wanted from her she couldn't give. She didn't want to give. She *wouldn't* give.

Before she lost her nerve, she said quickly, 'So now you know why I'm a career girl. And that won't ever change because I won't let it. I don't want or need a man in my life, Zak. I think it's only fair to spell that out, in case I've given you the wrong impression over this weekend. Nothing has changed in my mind. Nothing.' She stared at him defiantly.

He sat there, looking at her with his blue eyes, not saying

a word. After a moment or two her gaze fell from his and returned to the oak tree. There, she'd said it. Before things went too far. He couldn't say she hadn't played fair. All along, she had told him.

'Feel better now you've said it?' His voice was quiet, and she couldn't read what he was thinking in the measured tone.

No, she felt awful. Worse than awful. 'I just wanted to—'

'Spell it out. Yes, you've said.' The interruption was without heat. 'So, now you've done that, how about we go home and overindulge on Geraldine's beef and Yorkshire pudding before dozing the afternoon away in the shade of the garden—sound good? Maybe take the dogs for a walk when it's cooler?'

It sounded heavenly. Which meant it was certainly off limits. 'I need to get back to the flat, I've loads of work to do.' She forced a smile. 'Things that won't wait.'

'Which will be dealt with all the quicker if you've had a relaxing weekend recharging your batteries,' he said quietly.

Her batteries were fine, it was her libido she was having trouble with. Blossom made one more token protest. 'I've several hours' work waiting for me.'

'Tough.'

She was shocked into looking up. His face was expressionless, his tone pleasant when he said, 'I need to protect you from yourself, I can see that. I shall take you back after tea, OK? And Geraldine does a good old-fashioned high tea, complete with several different kinds of sandwiches and cakes, and home-made scones with lashings of cream and jam. The sort of country feasts previous generations took for granted.'

Blossom mentally resolved not to do open battle with Zak again. She couldn't win. He had an answer for everything.

'Don't you ever think of anything beyond your stomach?' she said tightly, aiming for acidity.

'Do you really want me to answer that? I wouldn't want you to run from the car screaming.' He grinned at her expression.

OK, she'd asked for that one. It confirmed it was futile to try and argue with him, though. 'I shall need to leave straight after tea,' she compromised. 'I'll be working all night as it is.'

'No problem.' In view of the fact he had just railroaded her into staying at his house against her will, his grin was insultingly unrepentant. So was his mouth when it took hers again.

His lips were warm and firm, stamping their claim on hers, and she felt too spent by her revelations about Dean—not to mention Zak's larger-than-life persona—to resist their sensual persuasion. They moved along her cheeks, her closed eyes, her ears. She shivered, capitulating fully to the sensations he drew forth with such effortless skill.

'This is real.' When she opened her eyes he was looking at her, all amusement gone. 'What we feel when we touch and taste. That can't lie.'

'Dean made love to me.' She hadn't thought about what she was going to say; it came out all by itself. 'And it was all lies.'

'Wrong. He had sex with you.' As she reared up against the harsh crudity, he let her shrink from him. 'And that was all it was. And, if you tell me that what we have is the same as what you felt with him, I don't believe you. Because I tell you one thing, Blossom—I've had women, more than I care to remember right at this moment, and not one of them has made me feel like you do. I've slept with them and experienced pleasure, but not one of them has made me feel what I feel with one kiss from you. Now, how do you explain that?'

'I'm…I'm a challenge.' Her chin lifted.

'Rubbish.' His voice was soft. 'Young lads who are still wet behind the ears might be turned on by a challenge; I left my teenage years behind some time ago. Before I met you, I admit all I was looking for was shared pleasure and satisfaction. I didn't want any clinging violets, no complications or messy entanglements that might end in tears. Just women of like mind who were happy with the freedom they had, freedom where they could choose to stay or walk away and we'd still remain friends. My childhood was an antidote against love. I saw what it did to my father. He loved my mother; however much he fought against it, he loved her at heart. Maybe that love turned to hate—he certainly wanted everyone to think so, but I'm not so sure. What I am sure about is that she messed up his life so completely there was no room in it for anyone else, not even his son.'

She sat very still, silent, not speaking. The look on his face was painful to see.

'And I told myself I would never allow such a thing in my life. That it would be the height of foolishness. I would make my way in the world by my own efforts, and I would carve out a future that *I* wanted. One where I had to consider no one, where I was as free as a bird.'

He paused, studying her face. 'Am I frightening you?'

Her throat was locked, she couldn't utter a sound. She wanted to say no, but it would have been a lie.

'I don't want to,' he said quietly. 'But the way I see it, you've made your views clear and I'm doing the same. It sounds the oldest line in the book to say you're different, but that's how I feel. I don't know what it is about you that hit me like a ton of bricks the first moment I saw you, but it happened. Just like that—wham. The door opened and a warm, tousled woman with food all over her T-shirt and something questionable on the side of her face looked at me with great brown eyes, and I was hooked.' He shook his head as though it still surprised him.

She didn't want him to say these things. This wasn't how it should have been. She stared at him, her heart thudding so hard it actually hurt.

'And I knew then I had to see you again. Whatever it took. I had to know.'

She didn't ask what it was he had to know. She wanted the conversation to end. If she went with this, if she got in any deeper, it would kill her when it ended. And it would end. A man like Zak was not for her; she could never keep someone like him. He met gorgeous women all the time, in his work, social life, *everywhere*. Sooner or later he'd wake up to the fact that he'd been mistaken, that there was nothing special about her. Of course, he wouldn't be like Dean. When it ended he'd be gentle, perhaps even sorry, but he would walk away and get on with his life, and she… She wouldn't.

'You're as white as a sheet,' he said at last. 'Talk to me.'

'I'm…sorry, Zak.' She forced the words out through numb lips. 'But I can't be what you want me to be. You have to understand that. It's not you, it's me.'

'I want you to be yourself, that's all.'

But that was not enough. It wouldn't be. The words were screaming in her head. She looked at him miserably. She would never be able to make him understand. He was so supremely self-confident, so sure of himself. They were aeons apart. 'I'm sorry,' she said again, turning her head away.

Outside the car there were people coming and going, couples, families, children darting here and there and being pulled back by harrassed parents. A normal day. For everyone else.

'OK,' he said after a minute or two had ticked by with excruciating slowness. 'So we go on as before. We get to know each other better without any commitment, if that's what you want.'

She didn't know what she wanted. 'I think it's only fair to you to call it a day right now,' she said flatly, as though the words weren't killing her.

He gave a faint little smile that held no amusement. 'I'm a big boy, Blossom,' he said quietly. 'I can take it. I don't want anything you can't give willingly. When you are ready to take the relationship on another step, let me know.'

'And if I'm never ready?'

Zak's eyes narrowed, and he gave her a long look. 'You will be.' Then he smiled, his voice lighter when he said, 'You won't be able to resist me for ever, believe me. I know.'

'Because you always get what you want?'

'That too.'

And on that enigmatic note he started the car, and the conversation was ended.

CHAPTER EIGHT

BLOSSOM returned to her flat fully intending to refuse all further dates with Zak until he finally accepted she meant what she said. But somehow it didn't work out like that.

Over the next few weeks she found herself seeing him more and more often, sometimes on fairly formal dates, when he would pick her up and take her to the theatre or dancing or for a meal, and other times they would just chill out at her place or his. She got to know Geraldine and Will better, and even Thor and Titus accepted her as one of their family, rolling over to have their tummies rubbed as soon as they saw her, and covering her in slobbery kisses given half the chance.

As the summer faded and a crisp, frosty autumn made itself felt, she began to find it hard to remember what her life had been like before Zak. She was constantly mad at herself, furious she hadn't the strength to stop seeing him, angry that he only had to turn up—all towering height and wicked blue eyes—and she was putty in his hands. He had determinedly woven himself into the fabric of her life, she knew that, so why couldn't she take appropriate action and break the threads?

He has no scruples, she told herself one wet Sunday morning as she sat having a coffee in her sitting room while the rain hurled itself against the window in ever-increasing fury. But then that wasn't true either. Look at last night.

She curled her feet under her on the sofa and breathed in the rich smell of the coffee.

Unlike this morning, yesterday had been a day of cold sunshine, crisp, crackly leaves and a high blue sky, and they had taken the dogs into the country and walked for hours, returning home late to one of Geraldine's steak-and-kidney pot pies. Afterwards she'd fallen asleep in his arms on the sofa, until he'd woken her to take her home by covering her face in kisses. One thing had led to another, but instead of carrying her up to his bedroom—something she had expected on other occasions too—he had stopped before things had gone too far. He always stopped. When she had looked into his face the question had been there in his blue eyes. The question he had never asked and which she didn't want to acknowledge. And so he had brought her home and they had both been left frustrated and unfulfilled.

She sighed, moving her legs irritably. It was her fault, she knew that. He had told her to let him know when she wanted to take their relationship to another level and, Zak being Zak, he had meant it. She sometimes caught him looking at her in an intense, hungry sort of way, but the moment he caught her gaze a veil would come down over his face, hiding his thoughts. The next move was up to her, she knew that too. He wouldn't make it. And she didn't think it was purely down to him being noble and waiting until she was ready, either. She had hurt his male pride that day in the summer.

What a mess… She stood up abruptly and walked into the kitchen, rinsing her mug under the tap and then putting it down so hard on the draining board she chipped it. She picked the mug up again and looked at the damaged surface—it was her in a nutshell. She didn't like that she was this way, but she couldn't change the person she had become in the last couple of years. She had tried, heaven knew she had tried since the summer, but at the bottom of her she was still waiting for Zak to get tired of her and it stopped her giving him what he wanted. At heart, she didn't trust him. It was as simple as that, really.

They couldn't carry on like this. Sooner or later he would get tired of waiting for something that wasn't going to happen, and things would get difficult. They would start to argue and get at each other, and she couldn't bear that. It was far better it ended now, cleanly and decisively, and in a way that brooked no discussion. But how? And would she be able to stand it afterwards?

The last thought brought her up short. None of that, she told herself silently. You were doing fine before you met Zak Hamilton, you'll do fine when he's no longer around. It was going to end one day anyway, you've always known that. This way is just so much better than a gradual decay.

She walked across to the little bureau where she kept all her bills and paperwork, and took out the letter that had come the previous morning. As she read it through again, she knew what she was going to do. She had known the very first time she had read it to be truthful, but she had put the decision to the back of her mind in order to enjoy one last day with Zak. Well, she'd had her day. Now it was time to be fair to both of them. They were going out for a drink that evening; she'd tell him when he came to the flat to pick her up.

Melissa phoned that afternoon for their usual weekly chat. Since she had been seeing Zak, they had met up twice with Melissa and Greg. Once when Melissa had had them round for Sunday lunch, and again one evening when Zak had treated them all to dinner to celebrate Greg's thirty-fifth birthday. The first occasion, when Zak had romped with the children all afternoon, had won Melissa over completely. Her sister had done a complete turnaround and declared anyone who could get Harry following them around like an adoring puppy *had* to be the genuine article.

'Children always know,' Melissa had said earnestly the next time Blossom had seen her sister on her own. 'They can spot a fake a mile off. And wasn't he *wonderful* with Harry? The girls too. And he was telling Greg he'd love kids of his own one day. I think he's ready to settle down at last.'

It had taken great forbearance on Blossom's part not to tell her sister she was talking a load of rubbish. Children didn't always know; why else all the warnings about not accepting sweets from strangers that parents the whole world over indulged in? Melissa had been doing what she always did— using any argument she could to support her point of view. Black would become white if Melissa wanted it to; she'd always been the same from a child. But Zak *was* Greg's boss, and if Melissa wanted to think he was superman complete with a pipe and slippers Blossom wouldn't say anything to challenge that. If nothing else it had made things easier for the present.

The present ended now when—after they had done the normal thing of her health, Melissa and Greg and the children's health, how well Harry and Simone were doing at big school, and the cute sayings Rebecca and Ella were picking up—Blossom had said, 'I've had the offer of a fantastic job in America. It will mean me being away for a couple of months, maybe three, but it's for one of the top designers and a chance in a lifetime.'

'Three months?' It was clear Melissa hadn't heard

anything else. 'But you can't be away for three months, not now, not with Zak.'

'I shan't be going with Zak,' Blossom said drily.

'You know what I mean. You can't leave him by himself for three months, Blossom.'

'He's not exactly going to be in solitary confinement.'

'Quite.' There was a pregnant pause. 'There'll be lots of women only too pleased to step into your shoes.'

'I'm a funny size. One foot is nearly a whole size bigger than the other, you know that. I usually have to buy two pairs to get one pair that fits, so I doubt anyone would want them.'

'Blossom!' It was nearly a scream.

'OK, OK. So you're saying as soon as I'm on the plane Zak will get out his little black book? And this is the man you're telling me is ready to settle down?'

This time the pause was longer. Then Melissa said, 'I don't mean that. I just mean…' She was clearly struggling. 'The temptation might be too much for him,' she finished weakly. 'Three months is a long time.'

'And for that reason I shall end things with Zak before I go.' She let the enormity of what she'd said sink in.

'I hope you don't mean that,' Melissa said after some seconds.

'I do, actually.' Blossom's voice was very firm.

After a pause that stretched for fifteen seconds this time, Melissa said flatly, 'This job is just an excuse, isn't it? A get-out clause because you're scared to death to take the plunge and admit you want to be with him permanently.'

Sisters. Who'd have them? Her voice thick with unshed tears, Blossom said huskily, 'I'm doing it, Mel. For whatever reason. I'm going to America, and I shall tell Zak not to wait for me. He'll be as free as a bird.'

'You're crazy, I mean it. Here's a man who's handsome, deliciously wealthy and ready to settle down—and not only that, he's mad about you. Anyone can see that. Why would you want to throw it all away? You have to get over Dean, Blossom. He's still ruining your life. Can't you see that?'

'I wouldn't have Dean back if he came in solid gold.'

'I know you're over him in *that* way, I didn't mean that. I meant…' Melissa sighed long and loudly. 'You know what I meant without me having to spell it out.' And then she did just that. 'He's soured you, made you cynical about men in general.'

Blossom didn't deny it. Instead she repeated flatly, 'I'm ending it tonight. I shan't change my mind.'

'There are times I want to shake you until your eyeballs rattle.'

Great. One hundred per cent support, there, then. 'I'm sorry, Mel, but I need to compose a letter and send it e-mail today to let them know I'm available and taking the work. I'll talk to you later in the week.' She needed to accept the job before she told Zak. That way she wouldn't weaken.

'Bye, then,' Melissa said unhappily. 'And Blossom?'

'Yes?' said Blossom warily.

'I think you're making the biggest mistake of your life, and I'm even taking Dean into the equation here. But whatever you do, you know I'm for you, don't you?'

The tears surfaced again and Blossom's voice was choked when she murmured, 'Thanks. I'll talk to you soon.'

By seven o'clock the e-mail had been sent, she'd had a shower, washed and dried her hair and was sitting in the flat waiting for Zak to arrive. She hadn't dressed up; there was no point, because after she'd told him what she was going to tell him they wouldn't be going anywhere. She felt sick and shaky, and when she'd tried to make herself a coffee to steady her nerves her hands had trembled so badly she'd had to leave it.

When the front-door buzzer sounded she jumped so violently her hands flapped out like a new-born baby fearing it was going to be dropped. She walked over to the intercom. 'Hello?'

'All ready?' Zak's voice came deep and smoky, and she trembled, her stomach turning over.

'Not really, I need to talk to you. Come in.' She pressed the release and then walked to her front door. When she opened it he was walking across the hall towards her. He was smiling, but it didn't reach his eyes.

She turned and walked back into the sitting room before he reached her and tried to kiss her, and when she heard the front door close she faced him. He was standing just inside the room, big and dark, his hair damp from the driving rain that was still hurtling down outside. She was glad it was raining. It would have made it ten times worse to do this on one of the beautiful autumn evenings the country had been enjoying before the current wet spell. Rain suited the pain inside her.

She half expected him to speak, to ask what was wrong, but she should have known Zak never did the expected. He simply stood and watched her, his blue eyes piercingly sharp like splintered glass as they glittered in the dim light from the one standard lamp she had on in the room.

'I need to talk to you.' She hated that her voice was trembling. She needed to be strong.

'You've already said that.' His hands were thrust in the pockets of his black overcoat, his head tilted slightly back as he looked at her. 'So, what's the problem?'

'Sit down.' She gestured at the sofa. 'Do you want a coffee?'

He nodded. 'Something tells me I'm going to need one,' he said drily.

He was standing gazing out of the French windows into the streaming courtyard, his back to the room, when she returned with the tray of coffee. He hadn't taken off his coat.

She placed the tray on the coffee table and gestured to the sofa again. 'Please sit down,' she said, pouring a black coffee and handing it to him once he was seated. She hoped he didn't notice her hands were shaking.

She sat down herself in one of the two armchairs, but didn't make the mistake of trying to drink her coffee, knowing she would spill it down her. Instead she handed him the letter. 'I received this yesterday,' she said quietly.

He put down his coffee, settled back on the sofa and read the letter through. Why it should have been that very moment in time that she knew she loved him she wasn't sure. But as she stared at his serious face, his long lashes shading his eyes as he read, it came in a blinding flash of revelation that shook her down to her toes. She loved him, and this love was nothing like the emotion she had felt for Dean. What she'd felt for him wasn't even a pale reflection of the flood of intense feeling that consumed her now.

She stood to her feet, saying hurriedly, 'I forgot the biscuits,' and made it to the kitchen where she buried her hot face in her hands. Stupid, stupid, stupid. How could she have crossed that threshold and let herself fall in love with him? She hugged herself round her middle, swaying gently in the middle of the room as she fought for control.

A blinding minute or so later, she grabbed the biscuit barrel and unceremoniously emptied half of it on a plate before walking back to the sitting room. He looked up as she entered. 'This looks like a fantastic opportunity,' he said evenly. 'Fashion shows in most of the major cities, high press coverage, lots of famous names involved.'

'It is.' Her legs felt like jelly. 'Chance of a lifetime.'

'Then you should do it. No question.'

She stared at him as she sat down. It wasn't the response she'd expected. 'I'm going to,' she said carefully.

'Good.' He placed the letter on the coffee table and picked up his coffee, drinking half of it in two great swallows before he said, 'After all, America isn't so far away these days. A few hours, and I can be with you most weekends. We can probably fit in an hour or two together, even if it's just dinner somewhere.'

No, no. The knowledge of how she felt, the power it gave him over her if he ever found out, was terrifying. She felt like a fly struggling in the sticky threads of a web with the spider about to pounce. 'That won't be possible.' She took a deep breath, her heart pounding so hard it made her ears ring. 'I don't want that. It wouldn't… I don't want that,' she repeated.

His face blank, he said quietly, 'What do you want, Blossom? What is it you're really saying here?'

'I think we ought to call it a day, finish things. You…you will be free to do whatever you want, as will I. It's the sensible thing to do in the circumstances. Long-distance relationships never work. They always go terribly wrong.'

'Really? How many long-distance relationships have you had on which to base that conclusion?'

The calm reasonableness of his tone didn't fool her. He was angry, she could see it in his eyes, and she couldn't blame him. She shrugged carefully. 'It's common knowledge.'

'Not to me.' He continued looking at her steadily.

'Zak, we agreed at the beginning this was going to be a casual thing, nothing heavy. I…I feel it's run its course.' Hark at herself, she thought sickly, parroting out the platitudes, acting as though they'd had nothing of substance between them when over the last weeks they'd revealed so much of their inner selves to each other. At least, he had. The thought jolted her. She had always kept something back.

'I don't believe you.' His eyes hadn't left her face.

'What?' She stared at him, taken aback.

'You're saying the obvious because the truth wouldn't sound so good.' He sat forward in his seat, his voice urgent. 'I've got too close, haven't I? You're in danger of letting down the drawbridge and you don't like that. The untouchable ice-queen is melting, and it's scared you to death.'

'That's crazy, I—'

He reached her in an instant, drawing her up into his arms and staring down into her face. 'Don't you know by now I won't hurt you, damn it? Haven't the last weeks proved a thing? We both know there've been a dozen times when I could have taken you and you'd have been willing, but I don't just want your body. I want all of you, Blossom. Everything. And if that scares you it's too bad. That's me. If I had wanted a brief affair I'd have bedded you in the first week, and I could have, make no mistake about it. But I want more from you than that. I always have. From the moment we met.'

Blossom's heart made a sickening lurch. 'I can't give you what you want. Surely you know that by now? I can't, Zak.'

'Wrong. You *won't*. That's very different.'

There were hundreds of women better looking than her, better figures, more witty, sparkling personalities, more experienced in all the ways it took to hold an intelligent, cultured, strong man like Zak. Why her?

She must have murmured the last words out loud, because now he said very softly, 'Why you? Don't you know that yet? I love you, Blossom. I've loved you from the first. Why else would I put up with you?'

She stared at him in numb disbelief.

'You might look like that, but do you think it's been fun to toss and turn the night away and have a dozen cold showers before dawn? To hold back, when everything in me has needed you so badly I can taste it? But if we had gone to bed it would have taken something important from you, I know that. I know *you*. You would have regretted it in the cold light of day, but having committed to such intimacy you would probably have stayed with me. But your *choice* would have been gone. Moments of passion would have led you into a position in which you were never secure, never fully fulfilled, never sure of me.'

He looked down at her, studying her face. 'I'm right, aren't I?' he said softly. 'When you make the decision to trust me with yourself, to stay with me, to accept I'm not like him, it has to be without sex clouding the issue. We both know we would be good together, but it was probably OK with him. This time there has to be more, and you need to make the decision to commit rationally.'

She swallowed. 'I've made my decision, and it's not to commit. I don't want to see you any more.'

'Just like that?' As she pulled away he let her go. 'I've just told you I love you. Doesn't that merit some response, even if it's "thanks but no thanks"?'

She nerved herself to go through with what she had decided. Her chin lifting, she said, 'It doesn't make any difference.'

'Doesn't make any difference?' he brought out in a stran-gled voice. 'Damn it, Blossom, it makes all the differences in the world.'

'Not to me. I've heard it—' She stopped abruptly.

His eyes narrowed. He stood looking at her, but now there was a penetrating, indecipherable expression on his face. 'You were going to say you've heard it all before, weren't you?' he said slowly, his voice tight and controlled as he made an obvious attempt to control his temper. 'Is that all it means to you? Well, let me tell you, you haven't heard it from me before. Neither has any other woman, if it comes to that. And if you don't know me well enough by now to believe it was damn hard for me to say that, then there really is no hope for us.'

Her heart was racing and there was a lump in her throat, panic, despair, fear and dread washing over her in equal measures.

'Your husband was a louse, Blossom.' Suddenly his American accent was stronger. 'He treated you like dirt and you didn't deserve it. But that was over more than two years ago.'

'You're saying I should have got over it by now?' she challenged, anger biting for the first time and providing her with welcome adrenalin. 'Put it behind me? Is that it?'

For a moment it looked as though he was going to deny it, and then he nodded slowly. 'Yeah. That's exactly what I think I'm trying to say. You've dealt with the fallout, and it's time to move on and stop acting the victim.'

She couldn't believe he'd just said what she thought he'd said. 'Victim?' Her body went rigid. 'How dare you talk to me like that?'

'Because it's the truth. At some time in their lives most people get a hit, be it illness or bereavement or betrayal, or whatever. There's no shame in being crushed, we're human, flesh and blood. But sooner or later you bite the bullet and get the hell back in there. I'm not minimising what you went through. I'm just saying that was then and this is now. If you live in the past the past is all you'll ever have.'

'I'm not living in the past.' Blossom glared at him. 'And I have moved on.'

'No, you haven't,' he said without heat, a strange sadness coming over his face. 'You look at me, and all you see is a man governed purely by what's between his legs.'

She stiffened at the crudity but he made no apology for it.

'You're not prepared to even consider that I can make what has gone wrong for you right. That I can deal with the hurt and rejection and wipe them away with my love. And I'm talking about love, Blossom. It has four letters—l-o-v-e, not s-e-x. Get that clear in your mind.'

She bit her lip. She had to hold on to what she had decided. She couldn't weaken. She must not. He was confusing her, making her doubt herself. Self-control was all she had.

'I know about rejection and loss,' he said quietly. 'They were my childhood companions, and they accompanied me into adulthood. They turned my father into a bitter shell of a man who was capable of great cruelty to his own son, and for a while it looked as though they'd stay with me for life. But I chose to show them the door, and when I did that I became free.'

His voice was very soft and gentle; it caused a physical ache in her chest that was overwhelming. He looked tough and strong but very vulnerable at the same time, and it was breaking her heart but the sense of self-protection was more powerful.

He might be right in everything he said, Blossom thought. She should stop dragging the past around like a ball and chain and discard the feelings of inadequacy and fear, and the hundred and one other emotions that paralysed her with regard to the future. And she had, to some extent. The therapy had seen to that. *But she never wanted to feel like she had when Dean had left.* She wouldn't survive it a second time. And she knew, knew without the shadow of a doubt, that if Zak let her down it would be a hundred times worse than what had gone before. So the possibility of that happening had to be dealt with.

'I don't think you're like Dean,' she said slowly. 'But you can't say how you're going to feel in a few months, a year, two years. No one can.' Her voice had an undeniable tremor in it, and she prayed she could finish without breaking down. If he held her again, if he kissed her, she'd be lost. 'I've got used to being on my own. I know where I stand that way. I fight my own battles and overcome my problems myself. I'm responsible to no one, and I don't depend on anyone. I have my home and my career, friends, family. It's enough for me.'

'No, it's not.' His voice was flat. 'And one day you'll realise it when it's too late.'

'Then that will be another problem I'll have to get over.' It sounded trite. She hadn't meant it to, but as she watched his face darken she knew he'd thought she was being flippant.

'And where does that leave me?' For the first time since she had known him, he was glaring at her in pure rage. 'I love you, and I know as sure as I'm standing here that what you feel for me is not some lukewarm emotion. If you gave yourself half a chance, you'd love me too. And I don't believe that rubbish that there's several partners in the world a person can fall in love with. I know what I feel. If you walk away you're giving us both a life sentence.'

He pulled her into him, kissing her with a desperate urgency that spoke of frustration and helpless rage. For a moment she almost weakened, wanting him so badly it seemed impossible she was considering sending him out of her life. He felt strong and solid and enduring, his fierce passion invoking an immediate response that was impossible to hide. Then she tore her mouth away, pushing against him with all her strength as she cried, 'Leave me alone, can't you? I don't want this, I don't want you!' Hysteria was in her voice.

He let her go at once, shaking his head in the manner of a boxer coming round from the knock out punch.

'Please go.' She had backed into a corner of the room to put some space between them, terrified she would run into his arms and tell him she'd changed her mind, that she loved him, that she'd take whatever he could give for as long as he wanted to give it.

'Hell, Blossom, don't look at me like that.' His voice was a growl. 'What do you think I am? I wasn't going to hurt you.'

But he already had. She stayed where she was, barely breathing, her face white and her eyes staring.

She watched him take several long pulls of air before he raked his hand through his hair and straightened his coat. And then he walked across the room without a word and opened the door, not pausing before shutting it behind him.

He had gone. Blossom's legs gave way and she sank down on to the carpet, shaking uncontrollably. He couldn't have gone, not like that.

But he had. The seconds ticked by in the silence of the room. She was alone, as she had told him she wanted to be. It had been the worst possible ending and it was all her fault.

CHAPTER NINE

THE night was endless, stretching interminably before it gave way to a cold, rainy dawn. Blossom had spent most of the night hours curled in an armchair in the sitting room in the dark, listening to the rain beating down, and endlessly going over every word she and Zak had spoken.

The telephone rang at seven o'clock just when she was making herself toast and coffee, and she leapt to answer it, her heart beating wildly. 'He-hello?' she stammered.

'Blossom?' Melissa's voice was pseudo-apologetic. 'I hope you don't mind me ringing so early, but I had to know. How did it go?'

Blossom shut her eyes tightly as the pounding in her chest subsided. Of course it wasn't Zak. Why would he ring her after everything she had said? She was so stupid.

'Blossom?' Melissa repeated. 'How did things go with Zak?'

'Not good,' she said briefly. Understatement of the year.

'As in little bit of tension, or more volcanic eruption?'

'Krakatoa, east of Java.' The film of the same name had been one of their favourites when they were little. They had always cried buckets when the lava had swept away the village.

'So it's over?' Melissa said disappointedly.

'Oh yes, it's definitely over.' To her horror the last word came out on a sob. She bit her lower lip hard.

There followed a great deal of cluck-clucking down the line as Melissa went into mother-hen mode, but eventually Blossom managed to persuade her sister she wasn't about to throw herself off a high building and finished the call. Unfortunately she didn't have any work that day; in her business it was often all or nothing, and today was nothing. The hours stretched endlessly before her, and she couldn't even go for a walk in the park with it raining cats and dogs. She sat limp and lifeless in the chair.

No. She wasn't going to do this. She wasn't going to slip into the frame of mind she'd had after Dean left, when for days on end the effort to get out of bed had been too much. She reached for her toast and forced herself to eat it, although it tasted like cardboard.

After breakfast she showered and pulled on some old clothes, and cleaned the flat from top to bottom, which took most of the day.

In the evening she received an answer to her e-mail: was there any possibility of her arriving a fortnight earlier than planned? Certain arrangements had gone wrong and it would be *such* a help. If she could fly out at the end of the week…

Blossom weighed up the couple of fairly mediocre shoots she had in the next week or two against leaving the country and escaping Zak's brooding presence in the flat. She e-mailed back that she'd be there by Friday, and then phoned one or two colleagues who agreed to take her shoots.

Four days later she was in the skies above Heathrow bound for the States, telling herself a new job was exactly what she needed. It would give her a different slant on things, focus her mind, keep her busy and bolster her self-confidence. It was good that Zak hadn't telephoned or tried to contact her in any way. It was. It really was.

From the moment she landed in America, her days were packed full without a moment to spare. The job was exciting, hectic and stimulating and, as the show moved from state to state with bewildering swiftness, half the time Blossom lost track of where she was. She needed all the skill and expertise she'd accumulated through the years to keep her head above water, but she managed it, more than holding her own with the handful of other top photographers on the job.

At night a few of them would sit in the bar of whatever hotel they were staying at, talking, playing cards and drinking. But finally would come the moment she dreaded and she would be alone in her room. More often than not she cried herself to sleep, but the next morning she would be up with the birds, all traces of the last night's tears gone when she presented a calm, cool and unruffled front to the world.

She resisted asking after Zak when she talked to Melissa for the whole of the first month. Then, after a particularly bad night when she had awoken in the early hours with the tears running down her face, her body curled up foetus-position, she knew she had to find out how he was. She acknowledged she had lost the battle with her subconscious.

She phoned Melissa when it was late evening in England and the children would be in bed. Her sister sounded slightly flustered. 'Blossom? I thought you were phoning again on Friday, not today.'

'I was.' Blossom paused. 'Is this a bad time?' she asked carefully. 'I can call later, if you're tied up right now.'

'No, no, it's fine. It's just that we have dinner guests, that's all. Is anything wrong?' Melissa added a touch anxiously.

'Not really, and I won't keep you if you've people there. It's just that I was wondering if you knew how Zak was. You haven't mentioned him at all.'

This time it was Melissa who paused. 'No, well, I didn't think you'd want to rake it up,' she said at last.

'I don't want to go over the whys and wherefores, if that's what you mean.' Blossom wondered how to put it, and then decided to just say it as it was. This was her sister, her twin. If she couldn't be frank and honest with Melissa, then with whom? 'I'm concerned about him, that's all,' she said quietly. 'That last night was so awful, Mel. You've no idea. I still feel so…' She ran out of words to describe the indescribable.

'Guilty?' Melissa put in helpfully after a moment or two.

She had been going to say something along the lines of 'miserable and lonely', but guilty was part of it too. 'I guess,' she said slowly. 'Among other things.'

'You know what I think. You've run away from him, Blossom. Taken the easy way out, instead of facing and conquering your gremlins. Of course you're going to feel rotten.'

'Thanks a bundle,' Blossom said drily. 'Don't ever think of joining the Samaritans, Mel.'

'Well, it's the truth.' Her sister's voice softened as she added, 'But I'm sorry you're feeling wretched.'

That just about described it. 'But it's my own fault, right?' Before her sister could answer, she continued, 'It's all right, I know it is.' The trouble was she'd found since she had left England, left Zak, that she couldn't think clearly any more. She had tried umpteen times to convince herself she had done the right thing, but it wasn't holding water. But when she considered the alternative it paralysed her with fear. So, either way she was snookered. Total no-win situation. The only logical, sane thing in her life was her work, and she had never been more grateful for it. It kept her focusing on something in the day.

She took a deep breath. 'So? Has Greg said how Zak is?'

'Not really.' This time the pause was even longer.

Melissa sounded cautious. Blossom's antennae pricked up. The good—or bad, depending on how you were looking at it—thing about being twins was that you knew each other through and through. 'What is it?' she asked flatly. 'What's happened?'

'What's what?' Another pause. 'I don't know what you mean.'

Definitely wary. 'He's not ill or anything, is he?' she asked as sudden alarm reared up. 'He's not had an accident?'

'Zak? No, he's fine as far as I know.'

Blossom closed her eyes, her heart beating in her ears. 'Is he seeing someone else?' *Only thing left.*

'Blossom, he's Greg's boss. He doesn't have to report his doings to us.' Melissa paused. 'I mean…'

'But you know something.' Melissa wasn't Melissa tonight.

'I don't.' Melissa sighed. 'I don't know anything.'

Blossom was not convinced. The more so when Melissa added, 'Anyway, correct me if I'm wrong, but didn't you tell me it was you who insisted you were both free agents now? He could be dating the whole of London and it would be none of your business any more. You signed him off good and proper, sis.'

She knew that. If anyone knew that, she did. Most of her dreams had featured Zak with someone else. 'It doesn't exactly help, you pointing that out,' she said tightly. 'OK?'

'Well, I'm sorry, but someone has to.'

They didn't, actually. 'I have to go.' She'd had enough.

'Oh, OK,' Melissa said cheerfully. 'Take care and ring when you can.'

Why? Pulling out her fingernails one by one would be more heartening. 'Love to Greg and the kids,' said Blossom stiffly before putting down the telephone.

She sat staring into space, helpless misery washing over her. He was seeing someone else. She knew it. And, like Melissa had so helpfully pointed out, he had every right to. Of course a sexy, virile man like Zak wouldn't sit at home twiddling his thumbs. She'd made it abundantly clear there was no future for them; he'd cut his losses and moved on. It was what people did.

Her heart contracted and she bit hard on her bottom lip. She wasn't going to ask after him again; that had been a *huge* mistake. He could run around with whomever he liked for all she cared. She got out her handkerchief and scrubbed at the tears coursing down her face.

The next weeks were just as hectic as the ones before the telephone call, but now, although she was exhausted each night, sleep was elusive. If she had thought she felt miserable before, it was nothing to how she felt once she knew Zak was seeing someone else. She couldn't sleep, she had to force herself to eat and although she was grimly professional, and the powers-that-be declared themselves delighted with her work, she got no pleasure or satisfaction from it. The last show finished five days before Christmas, and by then she was on her knees and had dropped two dress sizes. This would have been a bonus—she was at last the size ten she'd unsuccessfully aimed for since puberty—if she hadn't been so desolate.

It was useless to tell herself Zak getting over her so quickly confirmed she'd done the right thing, and that if he hadn't bothered to be miserable for a few weeks then she was well rid of him. It didn't ease the ache in her heart one bit.

She had studiously avoided any mention of him when she had spoken to Melissa. She'd kept all their conversations strictly centred on her nephew and nieces, and her work. Two safe topics. She could fill up talk time enthusing over the latter, and Melissa the former, and in between they'd discussed Christmas presents. Melissa had invited her to spend Christmas with them, and Blossom had accepted as always. The season was always difficult for her—Dean having chosen such a poignant time of the year to leave—and since her marriage break-up she had spent every Christmas with her sister, enjoying being part of a family.

She left America on the twenty-first of the month, and dozed from the moment the plane took off, thankful Melissa was meeting her at the other end. Once she was at her sister's home and could sleep her jet lag away she would be fine, she told herself in the odd moment she surfaced from the strange half-sleep her body had fallen into. And after Christmas she would pick up the threads again and get back to normal life. OK, so it would be a solitary existence, but that was what she had wanted. Answerable to no one, and no one answerable to her and able to tie her up in knots. Except he had. He was still doing it. But that would fade in time. It would have to.

On landing, it took ages to get through Customs. She stood feeling slightly sick and giddy as she waited for her luggage, and, by the time she was finally reunited with her case and equipment and various bits and pieces, she felt even more like a wet rag. She knew she looked like one too, which didn't help.

She hadn't bothered to put any make-up on for the journey home, knowing from experience it was far better to keep applying lashings of moisturizer, her skin being naturally very dry. Unfortunately, due to the fact she had dozed the journey away, she hadn't bothered to do that either. Now she was left with an irritably dry skin as well as no make-up—not a pretty picture, as the mirror in the ladies' cloakroom pointed out with neon brightness.

When Blossom walked through into the main terminal along with others from her flight, she wearily searched the crowd for Melissa. Then her heart gave a gigantic lurch and she stopped dead, causing half a dozen people behind her to do some quick manoeuvring with their trolleys and cases. Zak was standing there, very big, very dark, his vivid blue eyes meeting hers calmly.

'You all right, love?'

A big burly rugby type with arms like tree trunks stopped beside her, a small child sitting on the trolley he was pushing. There were notices saying this wasn't permitted, but Blossom doubted anyone would point this out to him. 'I'm fine.' She forced a smile. In spite of his bulk and the tattoos covering practically all visible flesh, his face had been concerned. 'Just getting my breath,' she added. That was true, but it had nothing to do with the weight of the trolley.

As the rugby player moved on, the dainty, tiny woman who was obviously his partner and the tot's mother at his side, Blossom began to follow them to the end of the roped-off walkway. Zak was waiting. For one crazy moment she wondered if he was meeting someone else before reason asserted itself. That would just have been too much of a coincidence.

'Hello, Blossom.' As she reached him he bent and kissed

her lightly, before taking charge of the trolley which had been determined to go its own way from the moment she had tried to push it. 'How are you?' he asked quietly.

How was she? She didn't have a clue; there were so many feelings coursing through her she didn't know which end was up. 'Fine,' she answered automatically through numb lips.

'You don't look it.'

She knew she didn't. If only she'd put some make-up on, done her hair, *anything*. 'It was a long journey,' she said stiffly. As though he didn't know. 'Tiring.'

He had begun to walk, and she had no option but to trot along at his side, her head whirling. 'Where's Melissa?' she asked after a second or two, realising that should have been her first thought.

'At home with her husband and children this time of night, I should imagine.' The deep voice was matter-of-fact, cool even.

She glanced at him but he didn't look at her, concentrating on the trolley and keeping his eyes in front. 'She was supposed to meet me. She didn't let me know she wasn't coming.'

She was stating the obvious, and his lazy drawl made this clear when he said, 'But I came instead.'

He was being deliberately obtuse, and scampering along like this trying to keep up with his long legs was putting her at a distinct disadvantage. 'I meant is anyone ill?' she said, her voice clipped. She couldn't keep up this pace.

'You mean besides you?' he said calmly.

'I'm not ill,' she said indignantly.

He stopped, looking down at her intently. 'Then I'm a monkey's uncle. You look like death warmed up, if you want to know.'

As hot colour rose into her face, Blossom told herself she

mustn't react. As steadily as she could, she said, 'Why are you here, Zak?' *After nearly three months of complete silence.* Not one phone call or letter. Nothing. Not to mention other women.

'Why?' With one hand he lifted her chin, looking down into her brown eyes. 'Why do you think?' And then he kissed her, a long, burning kiss during which they were both oblivious of passers-by. When his head lifted, he said, 'Missed me?'

The kiss had held her entranced—his kisses always held her entranced—but now Blossom stepped backwards a pace. What was this? He had the gall to kiss her, to talk in that soft, smoky voice as though she was the only girl in the world, when he had been off in pastures new? 'Zak—' She stopped, biting back the hot words. She had no right to object in any way; she had relinquished all her rights that evening back in the autumn. Instead she said quietly, 'I thought we were finished. We agreed—'

'I didn't agree to anything,' he interrupted equably. 'As I remember it, you were the one making all the decisions.'

He looked wonderful. He smelt wonderful. Blossom thought she had cried all the tears it was possible to cry, but now to her horror she felt more pricking the backs of her eyes. Swallowing at the constriction in her throat, she said huskily, 'Please don't do this.'

He continued to look at her for another moment, his eyes narrowing. Then he swore softly, taking her hand and keeping it beneath his on the handle of the trolley as he began to walk again. She had no option but to keep up with him.

Neither of them spoke during the time he paid for the car parking, after which they made their way to a gleaming Jaguar in one of the parking bays. Blossom didn't comment on the change of car, neither did she say anything as she watched him load her possessions into the ample boot and back seat of the leather-clad interior. In truth, she felt beyond words. This had suddenly turned into a strange dream, poignant, heartbreaking, painful. To see him, to be able to feast her eyes on him again, was both agonising and thrilling at the same time, and her emotions were just as raw as in the first moments when they had parted all those weeks before.

Once they left Heathrow, Christmas was suddenly all around them as the big car sped through the night, shop windows lit up with eye-catching garishness, and Christmas-tree lights twinkling in a hundred house windows as they passed by. And then the final touch came into being—it started to snow. Small, light teardrops to start with, but then big, feathery flakes began to fall out of a low, heavy sky.

They were like strangers, Blossom thought painfully as the silence continued to stretch and lengthen. Strangers who were awkward with each other and had nothing to say of consequence. Suddenly it was all too much. She wanted to bury her head in her hands and weep and wail, but instead she gazed out of the side window into the whirling whiteness beyond, willing herself not to speak. If he could keep up this silence, then so could she.

She didn't understand why he was here instead of Melissa. If she thought about it, he had sidestepped the question when she'd asked it very adroitly. Completely forgetting she had promised herself she wouldn't speak first, she said nervously, 'This isn't the way to Melissa's.'

'Who said we were going to Melissa's?'

'Me. I did.' She collected herself. 'I mean, that's what Melissa and I have arranged. I'm spending Christmas with them.'

He glanced at her, just one swift look, the street lamps

happening to light up the brilliant blue of his eyes. For an endless moment they were joined, something vital and potent quivering between them. 'I don't think so,' he said very calmly.

Bewildered, Blossom's heart began to pound with the force of a sledgehammer. 'I am.' Her voice sounded small. 'I am,' she said more strongly. 'I'm spending Christmas with my sister.'

He didn't reply, the car continuing to snake through the worsening weather, the windscreen wipers labouring under the increasingly thick snow. Already the ground outside the car was covered with a layer of white, the trees and rooftops taking on a chocolate-box prettiness.

'Zak, I want to go my sister's house,' she said loudly, glancing at his shadowed features. 'Stop this car.'

They had been travelling along a well-lit A-road and when he suddenly pulled into the kerb and cut the engine her heartbeat went haywire. 'OK, I've stopped it. What now?' He turned, his face expressionless.

'I want to go to Melissa's,' she repeated feverishly.

'No you don't.' He drew her into his arms, kissing her until she had no breath left. It was a confident kiss, passionate and warm. 'You don't,' he said softly as his mouth left hers.

Trembling, she said, 'This isn't fair.'

'I played by the rules and where did it get me?' There was no amusement in his face or voice. 'You walking out on me— that's where.' His finger outlined her lips, his eyes never leaving hers. 'And so now we play by *my* rules.'

'Which include kidnapping?' she shot back feverishly.

If she had thought to shame him, his lazy smile told her she could think again. 'Whatever it takes.'

She was too tired to consider her words. 'Don't pretend

you've been pining all alone, I know you haven't. I'm not a fool, Zak.'

'No, you're not a fool. Massively insecure, more insecure than I gave you credit for—to my cost—but not foolish. I haven't been seeing anyone else while you've been gone, Blossom. I know that's what you've been thinking, but it's not true.'

She stared at him. Something in his voice told her he was telling the truth. Shakily, she said, 'If that's the case, if you haven't been seeing anyone but you thought I believed you were, why didn't you do something about it?'

'Like what?' He raised sardonic eyebrows.

'Write to me, phone. You are the one who said America wasn't so far away these days.'

'And you were the one who said you didn't want me around while you were working,' he reminded her gently. 'In fact, you didn't want me around at all. Remember?' He smiled darkly.

'Then why are you here?' she said. 'Why come now?'

'Because I know you better than you know yourself. Sometimes you have to think you've lost something to value it.'

Her mouth went dry. 'You said you didn't play games. What's that, if not a game?'

'Strategic warfare,' he replied grimly. 'I'm fighting for our future, Blossom, yours and mine together. If it takes until I'm an old man with a long white beard, I'll continue fighting. I didn't plan on getting married with a Zimmer frame, but what the hell? I'm not proud.'

Her ears ringing, she stared at him. He had said *married*. Panic flared in her eyes. If she'd had the strength she would have opened the door and made a run for it. Yet there was no place she would rather be than here in the middle of a snow storm with Zak. But she couldn't be with him, that was the point.

Whether her inward confusion showed in her face she wasn't sure, but suddenly his softened, his voice a soothing murmur when he said, 'You're tired, worn out. You've lost weight and you look scrawny. You need some of Geraldine's cooking to fatten you up. That's why you're spending Christmas with me.'

As an invitation it could have been worded better. 'Melissa is expecting me to stay with them for Christmas. It's all arranged.' She stared at him helplessly. 'I've got presents.'

He grinned, suddenly very much the old Zak. 'On the contrary, your sister is quite happy to place you in my tender care. We've got to know each other well while you've been away, and I have her full approval. And we can give her the presents.'

Blossom's eyes opened wide. 'You've been seeing Melissa?'

'She and Greg have taken pity on a heartbroken man, if that's what you mean. Melissa seemed to think it was her duty to give me dinner at least a couple of times a week, and it would have been churlish to refuse. Anyway, I wanted to talk about you.'

Something clicked. 'You were there that night I phoned.' She stared at him, trying to remember what he would have gauged from Melissa's end of the conversation. 'That's why Melissa was so strange. I thought it was because—' She stopped abruptly.

'Because she knew I was seeing someone,' he finished for her. 'Yes, I gathered that much, trusting soul that you are.'

Her cheeks burning, she said defensively, 'That's deceitful, to listen to a private phone call.' Although he hadn't, exactly.

He didn't point this out, however. Instead he said very quietly, 'I was feeling like hell that night. It had been weeks and you hadn't mentioned me. Melissa was trying to jolly me along, but I was beginning to think…' He paused, then went on, 'And then you called, and from what Melissa said I knew you were still thinking about me.'

Still thinking about him—was he crazy? *All* she had done was think about him, day and night.

'I wanted to take the phone and talk to you, but Melissa wouldn't let me. And then she implied I was fooling around…' He shook his head. 'I thought she'd gone mad. But she assured me she knew what she was doing. You were her twin, she said, and she knew how your mind worked.'

'You mean she insinuated those things on purpose? Let me think you were dating again deliberately?' Blossom felt wounded.

'She wants the best for you.' He stroked the side of her face with one finger, before briefly touching her lips with his own. Then he started the engine, saying, 'And I'm the best. But you're too exhausted to talk any more now. I'm going to take you home and put you to bed, and you can sleep for as long as you want, OK? And when you wake up Geraldine will no doubt smother you with TLC. It comes from having no children. Still, it'll give those poor dogs a break.'

She wanted to argue, but she really was feeling quite odd. Light-headed and groggy, and so tired she felt shivery, but overall was the incredible knowledge that she was here with Zak. Going to his home. He hadn't given up on her. It wasn't over. And that was the best thing on earth and the most scary, because how would she find the strength to go through leaving him all over again? But she couldn't think about that now. Stress was starting to take its toll, and she was beyond analysing anything. Summoning all her will for one last effort, she murmured huskily, 'This is ridiculous. We're not seeing each other any more.'

'Then put this down to an illusion.' He did something to her seat and it tilted backwards. He reached into the back seat and fetched out a blanket, wrapping it round her before checking his mirrors and drawing on to the road again.

And, utterly worn out in body, soul and mind, Blossom slept. When they reached Zak's home she was vaguely aware of being helped out of the car, of Geraldine and Will, conversation, the dogs barking, but it was all dreamlike, chimerical, and barely penetrated the thick blanket of exhaustion. All she wanted to do was sleep. To escape back into that wonderful place where she didn't have to think or talk or feel.

Then she was in a soft, warm scented bed, and gratefully she let herself sink down and down through layers of darkness into nothing at all. And it was bliss…

CHAPTER TEN

WHEN Blossom finally opened her eyes and found her brain belonged to her again, she knew she had slept for a long, long time. She could remember stumbling visits to the *en suite*, Geraldine insisting she eat bowls of thick chunky soup with warm rolls, along with myriad cups of tea, but these were deep in fog and seemed like part of her dreams. They hadn't been, but neither had she been fully awake. Now she was.

She sat up in bed, aware she had one of her own nighties on. She couldn't remember undressing or sorting through her case, but she must have done. Unless someone had done it for her? She offered up a quick mental prayer it had been Geraldine, if so.

She reached for her wristwatch which had been placed on the table at the side of the bed and glanced at the time. Eleven o'clock. And from the light trying to force its way through the curtains it was eleven in the morning. Zak had met her at the airport about four o'clock in the afternoon, so that meant she had slept nearly twenty hours if she counted the drive to his house. She sat trying to orientate herself, amazed to find she was still tired.

A knock at the bedroom door was immediately followed

by Geraldine entering the room. 'Oh, you're awake, that's good.' The little face beamed as the housekeeper bustled across to the bed with a tray. 'You've had us all worried to death, although I said to Zak you'd just worn yourself out working so hard the last couple of months. Did it go well? Was it worth it?'

'What? Oh, yes, yes. I think so.' As Geraldine put the tray on her lap and bent and hugged her, Blossom tried to clear her mind. 'I'm sorry I've slept so long,' she said politely. 'If you'd woken me I could have come down to breakfast.'

Geraldine gave her what Blossom could only describe as an odd look. 'That's all right, dear,' she said. 'The doctor said to just let you sleep as long as you needed it, when Zak called him the first morning after you got here.'

'The first morning?' Blossom glanced at the tray. A bowl of soup and two fresh rolls along with a cup of tea reposed on it. She had a memory of Geraldine helping her to sit up and practically feeding her soup before she'd snuggled under the duvet again. Had that been once, or had there been more times? A note of alarm in her voice, she said, 'Geraldine, what day is it?' There was something strange here, something not right.

'Christmas Eve, dear. And a perfect one, I might add. The snow's a foot deep outside, but it's beautiful, crisp and white. No sludge. Mind, it's still cold enough to freeze your ears off, so you'll have to dress warm if you feel like a walk later.'

Blossom had only heard the first three words. Staring at the housekeeper in horror, she repeated, 'Christmas Eve? But it can't be. I can't have slept two whole days away.'

'And three nights.' Geraldine beamed. 'And I must say you look all the better for it. Scared me and Will to death, you did, when you first came in the door. And the weight you've lost! Not been on one of those silly diets, have you?'

Bemused, Blossom shook her head. 'No, I was working…'

'Do you remember your sister coming to see you?'

'Melissa? Here?' It was getting worse.

'She didn't stay long. Just wanted to satisfy herself you weren't at death's door, I think. She didn't think you were properly awake, but she sat and held your hand for a bit.'

'I can't believe this.' Blossom's voice was dazed. 'How can I have slept like this?'

'Because you've worked yourself to a state of collapse, that's how.'

The deep voice from the doorway brought both women's heads swinging round. Zak looked back at them, his hands thrust in the pockets of black denim jeans and a scowl on his face.

Blossom blinked. He looked as though he was furious. 'I didn't.' She stopped abruptly. She could hardly say it was her despair over losing him that had prompted the dramatic weight loss and sleepless nights. Perhaps better left as it was. 'I just did what needed to be done,' she finished weakly.

Geraldine tactfully withdrew, shutting the door behind her as Zak came further into the room. 'They clearly worked you to death, and whatever you got paid it wasn't enough. Damn it all, woman, can't you see you nearly pushed yourself to a breakdown? The jet lag probably saved you in as much as it tipped you into such a deep sleep.'

No, you saved me. He looked so big and dark and handsome in his black jeans, and white shirt open at the neck. A monochrome of pure maleness with sky-blue eyes. Her heart actually ached, she loved him so much. And he hadn't given up on her. She had done her worst, she'd walked away and told him there was no chance for the future, and still he had waited for her. What other man in the world would have done that? But she didn't care about other men. She only cared about him. She had treated him so badly and made them both suffer because she was terrified to trust again. She was still terrified, if it came to it. But, having tasted what it was like not to have him in her life, she didn't think she could go down that road again. So what was the alternative?

'How do you feel now?' He had obviously realised his sick-room technique left something to be desired. 'More like yourself?' he asked as he came to stand beside her.

She must have looked awful. Why was she destined to forever resemble something that had been pulled through a hedge backwards with this man? And why did he always have to look so incredibly good? Blossom swallowed. 'Amazingly, considering how long I've been asleep, I still feel tired,' she admitted. 'But I'm back in the land of the living, if that's what you mean.'

'That's what I mean.' His voice was soft, very soft, and possessed of a quality that made her cheeks burn. 'I've called myself every kind of fool the last couple of days for allowing you to drive yourself into the ground like that.'

She stared at him in astonishment. 'It wasn't your fault.'

He shook his head, moving the tray from the bed before sitting beside her. Cupping her face in his hands, he held her eyes as he said, 'It felt like it. Times were I nearly jumped on a plane and came to see you.'

She didn't deserve him. And it still seemed impossible that someone like him could love someone like her. But he did. It was crazy, incredible, but he did. She felt something falling away from around her heart; the shell was breaking, and it was part joy, part pain. The old panic was still there, but it was receding.

He kissed the tip of her nose and stood up, and she felt like reaching out and asking him to stay. But she didn't. She wasn't there yet. Instead she watched him leave the room and shut the door quietly behind him.

She left the soup where it was, flinging back the covers and padding into the *en suite* where she surveyed herself in the mirror. She groaned softly. If he could look at her the way he just had when she resembled a pasty, wild-haired creature that was plain scary, she had to trust he loved her, didn't she? She stared into the brown eyes in the mirror and they looked calmly back. Funny, when she didn't feel calm inside. Anything but.

One hot shower later she felt more human, and after drenching her skin in creamy moisturiser she dried her hair into a silky bob framing her face and falling featherlike on to her shoulders. The last show had been in New York, and one of the models had insisted her own hairdresser tidy Blossom's hair. He'd done a wonderful job, Blossom thought now, admiring the fact she had cheekbones for the first time in her life.

Once she was dressed she pulled back the curtains, letting out an involuntary gasp of delight as she did so. The trees and bushes were clothed in garments of white, which glittered crystal-like in the cold brightness of the winter sun high up in the blue sky. She could see where the two dogs had romped in the snow at some time, great canine footprints, and areas where they'd obviously rolled over and over marking the otherwise undisturbed purity. Suddenly she longed to be out in the fresh, biting air.

Picking up the tray—she was definitely off soup for the

time being, but could murder a ham sandwich—she left the room, only to become transfixed at the top of the stairs as she took in the scene below. The hall was dominated by one of the biggest Christmas trees she'd ever seen, a festive vision of scarlet and gold, with baubles, tiny flickering gold candles and red ribbon. Fresh red-berried ivy was entwined the whole length of the staircase, and somewhere downstairs Bing Crosby was crooning about a white Christmas.

On reaching the hall, she stood gazing at the tree for a few moments, turning as Geraldine came towards her from the kitchen.

'What are you doing out of bed?' Geraldine chided, taking the tray. 'We thought you'd get up later.'

'I feel much better.' It was true, she did, although slightly shaky. 'Geraldine, could I possibly have a sandwich rather than soup?'

The housekeeper smiled. 'You can have anything you want. We're so relieved you're on the mend. Why don't you join Zak in the drawing room? I was going to get lunch in ten minutes, for twelve o'clock. I'll call you through to the dining room when it's ready, or would you rather eat on trays in front of the fire? Being as it's Christmas Eve and all?'

This was obviously a great concession, and, feeling like an indulged child, Blossom said, 'On trays, if that's all right. Isn't everything beautiful? Do you always decorate the house at Christmas?'

Geraldine moved closer, her voice a whisper when she said, 'Zak likes it. I think it's something to do with never having Christmases as a child, not family ones, anyway. He's like a boy when we put the Christmas tree up, and there's another one in the drawing room with the presents underneath it.'

Blossom smiled back at the housekeeper, but she felt like crying. She couldn't bear to think of him as a little boy, unloved, unwanted. She'd had such a lovely childhood with her parents and Melissa, it had been everything it should have been.

As Geraldine bustled off back to the kitchen with the tray, Blossom stood a moment more looking at the tree. All that Zak had gone through could have made him a cold, bitter individual like his father, but, as he had told her before she had gone to America, he had chosen to let go of his past. And, if she wasn't going to ruin what they could have together, she had to do the same. He'd had a whole childhood and youth involving years of neglect and misery to put behind him; she'd had just seven months of marriage to a man who wasn't worthy to lick her boots. Zak was everything Dean hadn't been. Dean wouldn't have waited one day for any woman; he had been a man who had demanded slavish adoration as his right. For the first time since she had found out about Juliette, she found it in herself to pity the other woman.

Zak looked up as she entered the room, rising swiftly to his feet. 'You look much better,' he said softly, coming to meet her. 'There's colour in your cheeks again.'

'I feel better.' She glanced at the Christmas tree in the far corner of the room, which was only slightly smaller than the one in the hall. This one was decorated in green and white, tiny, glittering icicles and frosted-white baubles vying with garlands of green beads and tinsel. Beautifully wrapped presents in shiny silver paper tied with green and pistachio ribbons were piled beneath it, and the mantelpiece above the blazing log fire was draped with a thick twisted garland of holly. 'You like Christmas,' she said quietly, bringing her gaze to his. 'I can tell.'

'I like this one.' He reached out and drew her against him, his mouth covering her eyelids, forehead, cheeks, nose in small, burning kisses before he took her willing mouth. She lifted her arms and wrapped them round his shoulders, pressing into him, needing the physical closeness and the feel of his hard body against her softness. The kiss was deep, his tongue exploring the sweet intimacy of her inner mouth as he crushed her against him. Everything about it was right, they fitted together like two pieces of a jigsaw.

How could she have imagined she could live without his kisses? She had never known a kiss could be such an expression of intimacy until Zak had taken her lips. With exquisitely controlled sensuality he moved her against him, pleasuring her as well as himself as he wound their bodies into each other in a weaving, erotic swaying that had her straining against him in an agony of need. His thighs were hard against hers, his heart slamming against the wall of his chest, and she could feel the fine tremors shivering across the thickly muscled back and shoulders beneath her caressing fingertips. She breathed in the spicy male scent of him, intoxicated with pleasure.

'The taste of you is like a drug…' He continued to kiss her as he spoke, murmuring the words against her parted lips as he punctuated each word with a move of his hips. His hands splayed on her narrow waist before stroking up the sides of her body and moving to her breasts, rubbing the tautening nipples through the soft wool of her top with his fingertips.

Her nails were digging into his shoulderblades, and she moaned softly in her throat, oblivious of everything but what he was doing to her. He was breathing hard, the trembling in her body reflected in his, and she knew he was fighting for control even before he wrenched his mouth away, saying, 'One more second and I won't be able to stop. Do you hear me, Blossom?'

She heard him, but she couldn't do anything about it. It took Zak stepping back a pace and putting her from him to bring her out of the feverish spell he had woven on her senses.

She looked at him, studying his face as though she had never seen it before. Beneath black brows his eyes were narrowed with the desire which still had him in its grip, and his mouth was tense with the effort it had taken to stop their love-making. He looked hard and strong and ruthless as he stood there, and maybe he was when the occasion warranted it. But with her he had always mixed his strength with gentleness and understanding. Just like her father had done with her mother.

Two outstandingly handsome, charismatic men, separated by decades and destined never to know one another, but brothers under the skin in everything that mattered. How could she not have seen it before? Why had it taken months of misery and loneliness for her eyes to be opened? And what if he hadn't loved her enough to believe for them both?

'I love you.' Suddenly they were the easiest three words in the world to say. 'I love you more than I thought I could love anyone, and it frightens me to death.'

For a moment she thought he hadn't heard her because he didn't move, didn't speak, everything in him had stilled. And then he smiled, an incredibly sweet smile that broke her heart. 'That's my brave girl,' he said softly, reaching forward and drawing her against him again, but gently this time. He held her as though she was fragile and breakable, which was exactly how she felt.

They stood together in the silent room, the glistening world outside the window casting an ethereal glow over the surroundings, and the log fire crackling and spitting in the big grate. Blossom let the peace steal over her. It was Christmas Eve, after all.

Eventually, light years later, he stirred. Looking down at her, he said, his smoky, sexy voice sending warm shivers down her spine, 'I want you for my wife, Blossom. Nothing else will do. You do know that?'

She nodded. Finally she understood the sort of man he was. Loving her like he did, of course he would want the ultimate commitment. He was an all-or-nothing man.

'So, Blossom White, will you marry me?' he asked softly. 'Will you share my life and let me share yours? Will you be the mother of my children if we are blessed with babies, and will you love me all the days of my life as I will surely love you?'

It was every bit as terrifying as she had expected it to be. But he knew how she felt, she could see it in his eyes as he willed her to trust him and take the final step. 'Yes,' she said tremulously, holding on to him like grim death. 'Yes please.' He was her destiny. She knew that at last.

'And can it be real soon?' His eyes were violet-dark. 'I've waited long enough, and I can't wait much longer.'

She smiled shakily. 'You don't have to wait,' she said shakily. 'I'd marry you tomorrow if I could.'

'Christmas Day might be a bit of a problem, but by the end of the week there'll be a ring on your finger,' he promised evenly. 'And I'm not letting you out of my sight until then. Just in case.' His grip tightened to prove it.

She reached up, putting her lips to his. 'There's no "in

cases" any more.' Through a haze of tears she put her arms round him. 'I love you, I'll always love you. I'm not going to go anywhere unless it's with you.'

He heaved an unsteady breath. 'Now I know there's a Santa Claus.' And he kissed her.

The wedding took place on the day before New Year's Eve at a quaint little country hotel, the owner of which was barely able to conceal his delight at having such an event in the quiet spot after Christmas and before the New Year celebrations. It was a very small affair, but no less the charming for that. The function room had been decorated from floor to ceiling with fresh, sweet-smelling white lilies and baby's breath entwined with evergreens, the profusion of which turned it into an enchanted, perfumed arbour.

Harry was Blossom's slightly reluctant page boy, and Simone, Rebecca and Ella ecstatic bridesmaids. The three little girls wore fluffy silver and cream fairy-tale dresses that they spent most of the time twirling round in, and Harry was very grown up and serious in a little suit with a cream waistcoat and pint-sized cravat.

There were only four adults besides the bride and groom at the ceremony and champagne lunch to follow, but that was exactly how Blossom had wanted it. And Melissa, Greg, Geraldine and Will said it was the best wedding they had ever attended.

When Blossom walked down the tiny aisle hand in hand with Melissa she didn't give a thought to the stiff, formal register office service of three years before. All her thoughts were reserved for the tall, raven-haired man waiting for her at the end of the room. Her cream silk-crepe dress with a fitted bodice and a small train had been bought the day before, along with the bridesmaids' dresses and Harry's suit, but if she had searched for months she couldn't have found a frock more suited to her figure and colouring. She wore her hair loose and carried a small posy of one cream orchid surrounded by floaty feathers. Melissa was crying unashamedly as they reached Zak, but Blossom's eyes were shining with love, her fingers caressing the tiny diamond brooch pinned on the bodice of her dress which Zak had given her the first evening they had spent together. The last few days had been beyond wonderful, and now they had a lifetime of loving in front of them.

Zak had pulled every string in the book to get the paper-work finalised in time, and now, as the small bespectacled registrar began speaking, the speed with which it had all happened and the awesome vows she was about to make hit Blossom anew. And then Zak squeezed her hand and she looked into the blue, blue eyes and the world righted itself again. As it always would with him by her side.

The wedding lunch was a happy affair, the adults laughing and talking, and the children playing with the sackful of new toys Zak had produced to keep them entertained once they had finished their meal. Will had brought along his camera to film the whole proceedings, and Blossom was glad of this; she was so happy, so giddy and high on love, she knew she wouldn't remember half of the day once it was over. They were staying overnight at the hotel before flying to the Bahamas the next morning, where a friend of Zak had a sumptuous villa he was lending them for as long as they wanted to stay.

'Happy, Mrs Hamilton?' As she stood wrapped in Zak's arms on the hotel steps as they watched the others leave, a winter dusk was turning the sky into a blaze of red and gold, the colours reflected in the crystals on the snow like a carpet of precious stones. The scene was magical. The whole day had been magical.

As the cars disappeared she turned in his arms, the enchantment of the moment making her voice tremble as she whispered, 'Come to bed.'

'Have you no shame, woman?' he smiled, kissing the tip of her nose. 'It's not even five o'clock yet.'

'OK, then.' She smiled back, sliding her arms round his waist and snuggling into the hard male body. She knew he had been as impatient as her for their guests to leave. 'We'll have dinner first.'

'The hell we will,' he murmured softly.

The bridal suite wasn't large but it was beautifully fitted out in shades of ivory, cream and gold, the four-poster bed dominating the room. Zak had whisked her up in his arms and carried her over the threshold, and as he set her down, holding her tight against him, she could feel anticipation had already made him as hard as a rock.

He touched her eyelids with his lips, one after the other, before moving to her mouth. Her lips parted and his tongue took the territory within. There was a fire inside her, spreading to every nerve and sinew as the taste, the touch, the smell of him spun in her head. She felt she couldn't get close enough to him, and as he undid the zip of her dress her skin was alive from the tips of her toes to the crown of her head.

The frock slipped to her feet, and she stood revealed in the lacy underwear which—considering it was mere wisps of nothing—had cost a packet. It was worth every penny for the look on Zak's face as his eyes devoured her.

'My beautiful, beautiful wife,' he said, the wonder in his

voice making her blush. His hands moved to her breasts, stroking delicately until her nipples peaked beneath his exploring fingertips and her breath came ragged and fast.

She tugged at his shirt and undressed him as he peeled the last remaining slips of material from her body, and then they were naked at last. He was magnificent. She looked with something approaching awe at his muscled chest and shoulders and lean thighs, the dark hair on his chest narrowing to a thin line bisecting his flat stomach and then becoming thicker again between his legs. He was hugely aroused.

He drew her over to the bed, kissing and caressing and stroking her as he laid her down on the scented linen, and then he proceeded to take her into a captivating place she'd never been to before. Nothing she had experienced with Dean could have prepared her for being made love to by Zak. And that was what it was—being made *love* to. Her needs and wants were all-important to him, and instead of the quick satisfying of his desire he had begun to touch and taste every inch of her skin with delicate skilfulness, bringing her to the brink over and over again, only to slow her down and then begin the intoxicating art all over again. Sometimes playful and teasing, other times tender or lusty, he admired her with his eyes, his hands, his mouth, and with such erotic finesse she thought she would die from the pleasure he was creating.

'I love you, my darling, I love you more than life itself.' In the moment before he finally took her he breathed the words against her mouth. 'And this is just the beginning of a lifetime of love that will get better and better with each day that passes.'

'I know.' She clasped him to her, feverish in her desire that they come together at last. 'And I love you, so much.'

When he possessed her, even then his self-control held. He moved slowly at first, experimentally, watching her face to see her delectation as he increased the momentum of his rhythmic thrust. As he began to move harder and deeper, she felt a blindingly sweet sensation begin to grow until, as he possessed her to the hilt, she exploded into a world of light and sensation, and there was nothing but Zak and their love.

It was long moments before she could speak or move, and then her voice was husky as she held his face in her hands. 'Thank you.' She kissed him as they lay still joined together in the soft warmth of the bed, the tranquil frosted-pearl world outside the window quiet and still. 'Thank you for seeing what I couldn't see and believing in us.'

'A pleasure.' He smiled lazily, his eyes loving her.

'I never thought it could be like this,' she said softly. 'It was so…' There were no words to describe what it had been.

He kissed her, rolling over and then fitting her into his side as he drew the covers over them, his arm round her. 'Perfect,' he finished for her. 'Because we are perfect together. I've known other women, Blossom, but none of them have ever stirred in me what you did with just one look that first day. Love hit me like a thunderbolt, and the more I got to know you the more consuming it became. It was inconvenient, painful, demoralising at times…'

'Oh, Zak.' She kissed the side of his mouth.

'But I wouldn't have missed it for the world. I was only half alive till I met you and I knew it. I love everything about you, your warmth, your quirkiness, your sense of humour, your stubbornness, everything, because all the facets make up the whole. You're mine, you'll always be mine, because I will never let you go. I'll share you with our children, but that's all.'

Babies. Zak's babies. Warmth filled her, and she snuggled closer into his body, the rough magic of his body hair thrilling her. Determined little boys with black hair and blue eyes, and maybe a girl who would adore her daddy. He would be a wonderful father. Instinctive. You only had to see him with Harry and the girls to know that.

'I thought my future was all set out in front of me when I was in America,' she whispered. 'I looked down the years and they were empty and barren. I knew I'd made a mistake then, deep inside, but I would never have had the courage to do anything about it without you coming to get me.'

He gave the phantom of a smile. 'Hijacking you when you were too weary to fight me. It was the only way.'

She nodded, twisting in his arms and touching his face, tracing loving fingers over the hard planes of his jaw, and following the lines of his mouth. 'I never thought then I'd have a husband for Christmas,' she said, a little catch in her voice.

He kissed the tips of her fingers before pulling her on top of him, his body proving their love-making wasn't finished yet. 'I told you,' he said smokily. 'There is a Santa Claus after all.'

HARLEQUIN *Presents*

REQUEST YOUR FREE BOOKS!

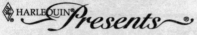 

2 FREE NOVELS
PLUS 2
FREE GIFTS!

YES! Please send me 2 FREE Harlequin Presents® novels and my 2 FREE gifts. After receiving them, if I don't wish to receive any more books, I can return the shipping statement marked "cancel." If I don't cancel, I will receive 6 brand-new novels every month and be billed just $3.80 per book in the U.S., or $4.47 per book in Canada, plus 25¢ shipping and handling per book and applicable taxes, if any*. That's a savings of close to 15% off the cover price! I understand that accepting the 2 free books and gifts places me under no obligation to buy anything. I can always return a shipment and cancel at any time. Even if I never buy another book from Harlequin, the two free books and gifts are mine to keep forever.

106 HDN EEXK   306 HDN EEXV

Name	(PLEASE PRINT)
Address	Apt. #
City	State/Prov.	Zip/Postal Code

Signature (if under 18, a parent or guardian must sign)

Mail to the **Harlequin Reader Service®:**
IN U.S.A.: P.O. Box 1867, Buffalo, NY 14240-1867
IN CANADA: P.O. Box 609, Fort Erie, Ontario L2A 5X3

Not valid to current Harlequin Presents subscribers.

**Want to try two free books from another line?
Call 1-800-873-8635 or visit www.morefreebooks.com.**

* Terms and prices subject to change without notice. NY residents add applicable sales tax. Canadian residents will be charged applicable provincial taxes and GST. This offer is limited to one order per household. All orders subject to approval. Credit or debit balances in a customer's account(s) may be offset by any other outstanding balance owed by or to the customer. Please allow 4 to 6 weeks for delivery.

Your Privacy: Harlequin is committed to protecting your privacy. Our Privacy Policy is available online at www.eHarlequin.com or upon request from the Reader Service. From time to time we make our lists of customers available to reputable firms who may have a product or service of interest to you. If you would prefer we not share your name and address, please check here. ☐

HP07

HARLEQUIN

Mediterranean NIGHTS™

A dangerous mission brings mystery and romance aboard Alexandra's Dream....

Coming in January 2008

FULL EXPOSURE

by

Diana Duncan

To the passengers aboard *Alexandra's Dream,* Ariana Bennett appears to be an unassuming librarian. But she's really working undercover to find the criminals who caused her father's death. Her snooping soon gets her into trouble—she is imprisoned at one of the ship's ports of call, but finds an ally in a mysterious stranger named Dante. Yet when their alliance turns to attraction, Ariana wonders if she can really trust him....

Look for FULL EXPOSURE wherever books are sold.